A
Country
Practice

New Beginnings

JUDITH COLQUHOUN

A Country Practice © JNP Films Pty Ltd

This novelization © Judith Colquhoun (2015) is based on 'A Country Practice' stories from the initial television series

Published 2015 by Corazon Books
(Wyndham Media Ltd)
27, Old Gloucester Street, London WC1N 3AX

www.greatstorieswithheart.com

ISBN: 1909752177

ISBN-13: 978-1909752177

Other titles in the *A Country Practice*
series coming in 2015

A Country Practice Book 2
A Country Practice Book 3

Read more about the series at
www.acountrypractice.info

PROLOGUE

The summer of 1981 had been long and hot in Adelaide.
People prayed for rain and watched the sky for signs of
smoke but neither had come – not yet, anyway. On this
particular February day the temperature was again
predicted to climb into the forties and already at six
o'clock you could feel the heat closing in, dry and dust-
laden. The young couple packing their over-laden
station-wagon smiled at each other, feeling they'd
chosen a good day to leave. There were mixed feelings
naturally, this city was home, but ahead lay a very big
adventure, a chance to re-invent themselves, the hope of
a new and different life. They were risk-takers, these
two; certainly not the sort to buy a suburban house on a
quarter-acre block and stay there in stultifying boredom
for the next fifty years.

Brendan Jones manoeuvred a last, very large box into
a space reserved for it, a space not quite large enough.
'What on earth *is* it?' he muttered.

'You know Caroline,' Molly laughed. 'I hate to
think.'

'Couldn't we just leave it on the nature strip?' A tempting idea but out of the question. Caroline was Molly's formidable mother. If she ever found out that her parting gift had not been duly appreciated, Molly would be disinherited. Brendan got the offending box into position at last and shut the rear door of the wagon. There wasn't room for a stray sock.

'Ready?' Brendan asked.

'Ready for anything,' Molly said.

And indeed they thought they were; certainly more than ready for the quiet little town in north-eastern Victoria to which they were headed. The question could also have been asked, was Wandin Valley quite ready for the Joneses?

CHAPTER ONE

Terence Elliott paused at the end of the last row of scraggly vines. There was fruit, yes, but not a lot of it and vintage was only a few weeks away. What the vines bore was evidence of long years of neglect. Still, Terence was an optimist. And if the house and the buildings were also in need of some repair, he was too busy enjoying the view away to the mountains in the east to take much notice. He smiled at the elderly woman who'd been his guide and extended his hand.

'Thanks, Mrs. Eldershaw. I'll let you know within the week.'

He walked back to his Nissan Patrol and headed off down the long drive, wondering if he were totally mad to even consider buying the place. Wondering too, how Mrs. Eldershaw must feel about selling when she'd called it home for fifty years. Terence couldn't imagine how it felt to put down roots like that, or to be forced to pull them up. He'd been in Wandin Valley for three years now and it was, he supposed, *starting* to feel like home. Certainly, the life he'd left behind in Sydney seemed further and further away, the disconnect more complete. But he could not see himself staying anywhere for fifty years. He got out to open the vineyard gate and a yellow Mercedes sped past travelling far too fast, Terence thought, it was a hardly a highway. He himself went in the opposite direction, taking a roundabout route back to Wandin Valley township; it was still early, time to make a quick house call on old Bill Jackson, see if he was okay after that snake bite. And then the hospital. Simon could handle surgery for a while. He grinned to himself; if the patients would let him, that is.

The yellow Mercedes, meanwhile, had been forced to a standstill by a very large mob of sheep. Sandra Myers, the woman behind the wheel, had left Sydney before dawn. She was exhausted and she was distraught. She beeped her horn but the man and boy in charge of the sheep, not to mention their dogs, ignored her.

She yelled out the window. 'Hey! Excuse me! You're blocking the road!'

There was a Commodore waiting behind her. Elaine Mackay, a local, got out and went to have a friendly word. 'I know it's annoying but they won't be long.'

'They're blocking the road,' Sandra said, uncomprehending.

Elaine smiled. 'You're in the country. Stock have right of way. Look, Jack's just moving them across into that other paddock, see? Won't take more than a few minutes and we'll be on our way.' She went back to her car. City people! What on earth was the rush? But as she would soon discover, Sandra Myers had reason enough to be in something of a panic.

At the Wandin Valley Clinic, on the other hand, where Terence Elliott and Simon Bowen laboured to keep the populace in good health, it was far too early in the day for rush or panic. In fact, neither was likely to affect

Simon, barring a major disaster. Simon was suffering as Terence himself had suffered when he'd first come to Wandin Valley. The locals, no matter how sick, avoided him. He'd asked Shirley Dean, the clinic's nurse and receptionist, about it and she'd told him plainly. 'For heaven's sake, Simon. You're new and very young. You're a city boy who drives a rather flashy sports car. How can you compete with old Dr Clarke?'

'I don't know, Shirl. What was old Dr Clarke like?'

'Sixties. Favoured tweeds and silk cravats. Played a lot of golf, member of Rotary. You know …'

Simon was getting the picture: he was no substitute for Dr Clarke, it would be years before anyone in this town trusted him.

But as he bounced into the clinic this particular morning and saw several patients already waiting, he thought for a moment that his luck had changed, that he had somehow assumed an aura of gravitas that had won the populace over. Not so.

'How long will Dr Elliott be, Shirl?' Esme Watson asked.

'I really can't say, Esme,' Shirley said. 'You could see Dr. Bowen?'

Simon gave Esme his most winning smile.

'I'll wait,' said Esme.

'Sorry,' said Shirley sotto to Simon.

Simon hid his disappointment. 'Lovely roses, Sister.'

'She's got a secret admirer.' This from Harry Palmer.

Shirley said quickly, 'They're from Sergeant Frank Gilroy. In appreciation of my many kindnesses to his late wife.'

Simon was reading the card. 'It just says, "Warm regards, Frank Gilroy".' Shirley snatched it out of his hand.

'Best part of a year, isn't it? That Frank's wife's been dead?'

Harry should have kept quiet. Shirley smiled sweetly and stood up. 'You can pop into doctor's room now, Mr Palmer. I'll be giving you your injection today.'

Simon murmured, 'Can I …?'

'No, no. It'll be my pleasure.'

Simon grinned and helped himself to one of her roses, which he stuck in his lapel. Shirley took pity on him. 'You do have someone at ten fifteen. Jenny Secombe.'

'A real live patient? Me? I will try to compose myself.'

He went off into his surgery.

Sandra Myers was not composed. When Jack Dale's sheep had finally cleared the road, she had taken off too fast again, relying on the German engineering under the bonnet to keep her safe. It could only do so much. Sandra was tired and in pain and her reflexes were not as good as usual. She misjudged a bend on this unfamiliar road and skidded off into the gravel. No major damage was done but she was badly shocked. Elaine Mackay, arriving some time later, found her there with her head on the steering wheel, weeping.

'I'll call an ambulance.'

'No, I'm alright. I'm just – upset.'

'What happened?'

'I took the bend too quickly. Stupid.'

Elaine felt something wasn't quite right. 'Where are you going in such a hurry?' she asked.

'I was heading for Melbourne but I turned off – ' She gasped in sudden pain.

Elaine was all concern. 'What is it?' Suddenly she noticed the seat belt stretched over Sandra's enlarged belly. 'Good God, you're not in labour?'

'I think I must be. It's early. There was a sign – something Valley? I thought I'd better find a doctor.'

'Wandin Valley. We've got a really good little

hospital. You shouldn't be driving though, I'll take you.'

'Thanks, but it's not that far, is it? I can manage.'

Elaine doubted that she could but Sandra sounded determined. 'It's about ten kilometres. At least let me show you the way. I'm Elaine Mackay, by the way.'

'Sandra. Sandra Myers.'

'Follow me, Mrs. Myers.' Elaine smiled. 'We'll take it a bit slower if that's okay.' She drove off sedately, wondering what on earth this young woman was doing so far from home, so large with child – and so very much alone.

Terence Elliot was in the office of the Wandin Valley Bush Nursing Hospital, on the phone to Shirley Dean, when Elaine brought Sandra in and sat her down. Elaine had a quick word with Marta Kurtesz, the matron.

'Name's Sandra Myers. I found her not far from the Widgeera turnoff, she'd driven all the way from Sydney. Skidded off the road. Labour started about three hours ago.'

On the phone, Terence said to Shirley, 'Sorry Shirl, something's come up, I may be a bit longer than expected. Tell them they *have* to see Simon!' He hung up.

'I'm late for a meeting,' Elaine was saying, 'can I leave her with you then?'

'Yes, of course, and thanks Elaine.' Marta already had an arm around Sandra.

'Good luck, Mrs. Myers!' And Elaine was gone.

'She was very kind,' Sandra said.

'She's a powerhouse,' Terence told her. 'Does all our fund-raising.' But Sandra was having another contraction and didn't comment. In fact she said very little at all while they got her to a room and Marta helped her into a hospital gown and into bed. Then Terence examined her.

'Your first baby?'

Sandra nodded. 'It's not due for another month.'

'You're sure about your dates?'

'Absolutely.'

'And you've not had any spotting or bleeding?'

'Nothing at all. It's too soon, isn't it? Can't you stop it?'

'Not really, Mrs. Myers. Your baby's decided now's the time. Elaine said you'd driven from Sydney?'

'Yes.'

'So your own doctor's there?'

Sandra nodded.

'I can at least give him a call then. And your husband?'

'No!' Sandra's vehemence surprised even her. She said again, more quietly, 'Please ... no.'

Terence smiled. 'Your choice.' He sensed there was more going on here than they knew about as yet and he wanted her as calm and relaxed as possible. She had another contraction then and handled it well, breathing deeply to combat the pain. Sandra had clearly been to ante-natal classes. Marta checked her watch. Twenty second contractions every five minutes. There was certainly no stopping this baby.

Sandra asked how long she'd have to stay in hospital and was told a week or so. The news did not seem to upset her too much. Marta asked where she was heading. Sandra hesitated.

'Melbourne. For now, anyway.'

Marta and Terence both thought it a strange answer; not to know where you were going with a newborn baby. But it was none of their business.

'I really should get to the surgery. I'll drop back later, Mrs. Myers, and see how you're going. Matron Kurtesz can phone me if there are any developments. Oh – your doctor's name?'

'Dr. Lionel Cohen. He's in Double Bay. I can't remember the number.'

'I'll find him, don't worry.'

Sandra just nodded. She was looking tired now.

Terence added, 'Just try to get some rest.'

Marta asked, 'Do you have any luggage, Mrs Myers, maybe I could get it for you?'

'In the car. The keys are in my handbag.' Marta retrieved them. 'It's a yellow Mercedes.'

Terence, waiting in the doorway, reacted to this but neither woman noticed. Sandra said again, anxiously, 'Please. Promise me you won't tell my husband where I am? I don't want him here.'

Marta tried to reassure her. 'It's your decision entirely, Mrs. Myers.'

Sandra turned away then and Marta walked outside with Terence. It had turned into a glorious, if hot, autumn day. Marta regretted that she was unlikely to get a chance to go for a ride, the way things were panning out. She made a mental note to ring the stables and make sure that someone else gave The General a work out. Terence was looking at Sandra's Mercedes.

'I was out at Mrs. Eldershaw's this morning. That thing passed me like it was on the autobahn.'

'She's troubled about something. Elaine also said she was driving too fast, she'd actually run off the road.'

'See if you can find out what going's on, Marta? Why she's driven alone from Sydney and washed up here.'

'You're worried about the baby?'

'I am, a little. She's a small woman with a small pelvis … a highly emotional state is not going to help her. Find out what she's running away from.'

Marta laughed at that. 'A man, of course. What else? By the way – what were you doing out at Mrs. Eldershaw's? Did you try any of their wine?'

'There's been no wine made there for ten years. Not

since her husband died. Sad really. I did admire the view, though. You can see clearly all the way to Mt Tallebung. Fantastic.'

He drove off, giving her a wave. Marta smiled. She wondered what he really thought of the place and whether he would indeed buy it, or anywhere else for that matter. Marta had got to know Terence quite well, she saw a little of herself in him for the past still haunted them both. She wasn't sure that growing grapes would lay the ghosts to rest. She went to retrieve Sandra's belongings from the Mercedes.

Outside the clinic, Jenny Secombe, who'd never been in a Mercedes in her life, was parked with her boyfriend, Tony Pieri, in Tony's beaten up panel van. This was the vehicle that Jenny's father privately thought of as the sin bin, even whilst fervently hoping that his daughter committed no fall from grace within it. Jenny was nervous about this landmark visit to the doctor and rather wished she'd come alone; she didn't need Tony making things worse.

'I'll come in too if you like.' He almost had to yell over the sound of Rick Springfield belting out *Jessie's Girl* on the cassette-player. Jenny leaned over and turned it off. It was a good song but she thought the occasion deserved a bit more solemnity. 'If you're nervous.'

'I'm not nervous. Well just a bit. And you'd only get embarrassed.'

'No I wouldn't.'

Jenny started to get out of the car. 'Don't wait. I'll see you tonight.'

'Hey! What if your father finds out?'

'How could he? Doctors are like priests. Sworn to secrecy.'

'You hope.' He grinned at her. He had the best smile. It was the one of the things she loved about him. He was her first real boyfriend. She loved everything about him.

Jenny walked off towards the clinic entrance. As Tony started the car, a hand grabbed the steering wheel.

'Hey, Pieri, what's doin'?'

Peter bloody Gleeson. Three years older than Tony, he'd been picking on him since primary school.

'Nothing.'

'Dropping your girlfriend off at the doc, Tone, what's that all about?'

'None of your business, Pete.'

'I'm just concerned about her, mate. Real concerned.'

'Got the flu, hasn't she?'

'The flu?' Peter laughed. 'You sure you haven't got her up the duff?' He left then, still laughing, leaving Tony seething but knowing better than to go after him. You always came off second best with people like Peter Gleeson. 'Should have been drowned at birth' was Tony's uncharitable character assessment and many – Sergeant Frank Gilroy included – might have agreed.

CHAPTER TWO

Shirley Dean was on the phone when Jenny entered the clinic. 'Thursday at twelve, Alma, that's the best I can do. Or you could see Dr Bowen this afternoon.' Shirley rolled her eyes in exasperation. 'Alma, that's ridiculous. What if it's appendicitis? It could be peritonitis by Thursday. Come in at four-thirty and see Dr. Bowen, I'll send the ambulance if you don't turn up.' She hung up, shaking her head and smiled at Jenny. 'Dr Bowen won't be a minute, Jenny.'

Jenny looked rather uncertainly at the other patients.

'Oh, they're all waiting for Dr. Elliott.'

'I thought I'd be seeing Dr. Elliott,' Jenny said.

'Not unless you want to wait till Thursday,' said Shirley.

Jenny gave it a moment's consideration and shook her head. 'I guess Dr. Bowen'll do.' She took a seat.

'Bravo,' said Shirley. 'A pity some of our other patients don't share your adventurous spirit.'

She ignored the glares which some of the 'other' patients gave her. Terence chose that opportune moment to finally arrive. He greeted all and sundry. 'Sorry to have kept you. Bit of an emergency.' He went to Shirley's desk. 'Morning, Sister Dean. Any calls from the hospital, put them straight through?'

'Certainly, doctor.' Shirley handed him the record card for his first patient.

'Thanks,' Terence said. 'Nice roses.' Shirley gave him a look.

'Mrs. Anderson?' Terence called, just as Simon Bowen came out to see if he had a patient yet. 'Sorry I'm late,' Terence said. 'But you could have cleared the decks for me.'

Simon was not amused. 'We need an outbreak of plague. Then they'd have to trust me.'

'Ah, Dr Bowen,' said Shirley. 'Miss Secombe's here.' She nodded to Jenny who got up again. Simon ushered her into his consulting room as if she were royalty, took her card from Shirley and shut the door.

'Wonder what she's doing here?' Esme Watson enquired of the room in general.

'Perhaps she's feeling unwell, Esme.'

'Doesn't look sick, does she? Ought to be in school.' Esme sniffed and managed to imply that Jenny Secombe was somehow, by appearing at the clinic in school hours, up to no good.

Simon Bowen was leading Jenny herself through her meagre medical history. 'Your last visit was three years ago, Miss Secombe? Good heavens, a poor GP would starve to death if he had too many patients like you.'

Jenny smiled, she thought Dr Bowen wasn't so bad after all. 'You can call me Jenny, doctor.'

'Thank you. I see Dr Clarke prescribed Intal for your asthma. Are you still taking it?' Jenny shook her head. 'No more attacks?'

'Just seemed to stop having them.'

'Well let's hope you stay stopped. So what brings you

here today?'

There was a pause and then Jenny came right out with it. 'I want to go on the pill,' she said.

Not quite what Simon was expecting but he gave no sign of surprise. 'I see,' he said. 'The contraceptive pill.'

'Yes.'

Simon glanced at her card. 'And you haven't been on it before?'

'No.'

Simon reached for his sphygmomanometer. 'There are some risks with the pill, Jenny. I'll need to give you a full physical examination first. Blood pressure, that sort of thing.'

'Fine.'

'What sort of contraception have you been using?'

'None. That is … you know. I haven't …'

Simon got the picture. 'That's okay. You've decided to have a physical relationship and you want to go on the pill. Very sensible. You've got things in the right order. A lot of people do it the other way –'

Just when he thought it was all going quite well, the phone rang. It was Shirley, talking in a whisper – prompted by Esme's comment about how Jenny should have been at school.

'Sorry, Simon. But I'm not sure it's on her card. And you ought to know. Jenny's only fifteen.'

Simon was stunned and tried not to look at Jenny. He had her down for seventeen, eighteen even. 'Thanks, Sister. Tell him I'll be there as soon as I can.' He hung up, smiled at Jenny.

'Sorry about that, we were just doing your blood pressure, weren't we?' He continued, chatting while he did so. 'Now – never been on the pill before?'

'No. I told you.'

'No trouble with your periods? Pain, heavy bleeding, irregularity?'

'No, nothing. I'm really lucky.'

'Blood pressure's fine. How old are you, Jenny, there's no date of birth on your card.'

'Fifteen.'

Simon sighed. He sat down at his desk. 'We've got a bit of a problem.'

'Why?'

'Jenny, I can't prescribe the pill without your parents' permission.'

'*What*?' She was dumbfounded.

'I'm sorry. If you had irregular periods, something like that, I could maybe give it to you for medical reasons. But you don't. And you're under the age of consent. There are laws about these things.'

'It's crazy!'

'Well maybe not. It's a big step, you should really talk it over with someone – like a parent.'

'There's just my father. He'd never understand.'

'Would you like me to talk to him?'

'No! That'd just make it worse.'

'When do you turn sixteen?'

'Next January.'

'That's not so long.'

'You don't understand. I'm in love with this boy. He loves me. I can't expect him to wait till then, can I? *I* don't want to wait.'

'I'm really sorry.'

'Are you, Dr Bowen? Sorry enough to do the abortion if I get pregnant?'

Close to tears, she rushed out of the room. Simon sank back into his seat, defeated. In the reception area, Esme Watson watched Jenny dash out and tut-tutted. 'You do wonder, don't you?' Esme said.

Shirley smiled sweetly. 'Perhaps she needs some fresh air, Esme. Feel a bit that way myself.' But instead of following Jenny she went into Simon's consulting room.

'You okay?'

'You just saved my life, Shirl. Jenny Secombe wanted to go on the pill.'

'Thought that might have been it. Lovely kid but she's hanging out with Tony Pieri.'

'Something wrong with him?'

'He's a teenage boy, Simon. Surely you can remember.'

'Remember? Nothing's changed!'

'Oh please. Half the females around here are lusting after you.'

'Not the right half,' Simon said, thinking of Shirley's daughter, Vicky, the local vet, who continually rejected his advances. He sighed. 'Right now, I'm wondering why I ever came here, Shirl. I let that kid down badly.'

'You had no choice. Come on Simon, you'll get a chance to do your bit before long.' Prophetic words, as things turned out.

At the hospital, Sister Judy Loveday was discussing the newest admission with Matron Kurtesz.

'I thought she might open up to you a bit,' Marta said. 'You're more her age.'

'Not a hope. She just lies there and cries.' Judy was a fine nurse but not known for her sensitivity. 'Won't say what the matter is, either. I mean, honestly, Matron, what does it take to make some people happy?'

'Meaning?' Marta asked.

'Well – she's got a baby on the way, there's a Merc out the front and as for the clothes, the shoes, the jewellery … she's loaded, that's obvious.'

But designer labels don't make for easier labour and Judy was in fact worried about Sandra Myers. Her contractions were closer together but there was no sign of second staging and the baby's head was still high.

'I'd better check her out myself,' Marta said. 'Can

you look in on Mr. Robinson, see if he feels like getting up for a while?'

'Will do. Where's the husband, by the way?'

'A very good question,' Marta said as she headed to Sandra's room.

Marta had to admit that Judy was right about Sandra Myers, the signs of money – and good taste – were there in all her possessions. She decided to try once more to get through to her.

'I'm afraid the entire staff have been out to ogle your car, Mrs. Myers. It really is beautiful. And great fun to drive, I'm sure.'

Sandra realised she was trying to be friendly and reached for the box of tissues by the bed. Marta passed them to her. 'It was a birthday present,' Sandra said. 'Last month. I was twenty-eight.'

'Lucky you.'

'You think so?'

Marta smiled. 'I wouldn't mind being twenty-eight again. How are those contractions now?'

'A bit more frequent.' Marta prepared to take her blood pressure. 'Is something wrong?'

'No, not at all. But I think we might get Dr Elliott back to have another look at you.'

'He's not an obstetrician, is he?'

'He's very competent, Mrs. Myers. You can trust him to look after your baby.' She paused for a moment. 'A new baby – it's usually a time of joy. But you are very unhappy.'

'I have reason to be.'

Marta sighed. She was having no more luck than Judy Loveday in getting through to this young woman.

CHAPTER THREE

In the flat above the clinic, Terence was trying to get through to Simon. 'I admit it's a really tough situation, Simon. But you did the right thing.'

'Exactly what I said.' Shirley had made tea and passed them both a cup.

'Thanks, Shirl. So I refuse the pill – what if she now goes off and gets pregnant?'

'Not your responsibility. She's got a family, Simon, that's what they're for.'

Shirley said, 'Actually, she's only got a dad.'

'So presumably she's gone off to ask him for permission.' Terence smiled. 'Poor guy.'

'I thought she was at least sixteen,' Simon said. 'Maybe more. It was Shirley who put me straight.'

'Just as well,' Terence said. 'If you'd gone ahead and her dad had found out, he could have sued you for contributing to the delinquency of his daughter.'

Simon grinned. 'How quaint and old-fashioned.' Then it hit him. 'Though I suppose I'd end up with even fewer patients than I'm getting now.'

Terence looks at Shirley. 'Surely you've told him?'

'I've told him.' She turned to Simon. 'Terence had one patient in the first two weeks. Just one. Look at him now. Universally adored.'

The phone rang and Terence went to answer it. 'It'll be the hospital,' Shirley said.

Simon still sounded plaintive. 'I'd settle for being just a little bit adored.'

'Sorry, that was Marta. Got to dash.'

'I can't help?' Simon asked, hope in his heart.

Terence shook his head. 'No, employ your winning ways at afternoon surgery, I could be a while.' And he was gone, leaving Simon disconsolate.

'He doesn't trust me.'

'Rubbish, darling, there's a problem, that's all.'

'One Matron Kurtesz? I find her a problem too.'

Shirley laughed. 'Better men than you have tried and failed.'

'What's wrong with her?'

'Nothing's wrong with her! Why should every single woman be panting after a male?'

'So Sergeant Gilroy's wasting those beautiful roses?' Shirley just gave him her death stare. Simon had the good grace to back down. 'Sorry! But Terence ... he's divorced, right?'

'I'm honestly not sure. He does go to Melbourne once a month but why, I don't know. Now I really must do my shopping.'

'One more thing – do you know where I can borrow a dog?'

Shirley stared at him in amazement.

'You want to borrow a dog?'

'Just for a few hours. It'll get a free check-over by a qualified vet.'

It dawned on Shirley then what he was up to. She started to laugh.

'You con-man! Why not pick up the phone and ring her?'

'I've tried. She just says no. I don't suppose you'd put in a good word for me?'

'Simon,' said Shirley, 'anyone I recommended, my daughter would run a mile from.'

But Simon refused to be discouraged. 'Just a tiny little dog?'

He looked so pitiful that Shirley reconsidered.

'Maybe there is one.'

Back downstairs in the clinic, Shirley handed Simon a patient card. 'When you've got a minute? It's just a repeat prescription.'

Simon read it. 'Migraine? In a sixteen-year-old boy?'

'Tim Bourke, poor kid. He's had it for years. His mum usually gets a six-month's supply.'

Simon wasn't too keen about that. 'I don't like just writing prescriptions, not when he's had an illness for four years! Can you get him in to see me?'

'Of course. I'll just have to find a way to convince his mum. Since old Dr Clarke never had a problem with it. On the other hand – if you can turn out to be a miracle-worker, she's the sort who'll sing your praises all over town.'

Simon liked the idea of a challenge. He could see patients queuing for his services all the way down the path. 'I'll do it. I'll cure that boy.'

'Good luck. But do be warned – Dr Clarke gave it his best shot. No one likes to see a kid with chronic migraine.'

Like all first-time mothers, Sandra Myers was learning that labour is not for the faint-hearted. It had been going on for several hours now and despite the kindness of strangers in this little bush hospital stuck in the middle of nowhere, or rather in a pretty river valley in southeastern Australia, she felt she was rapidly reaching the limits of her endurance. She was exhausted, restless and sweating profusely and her pulse rate was up. Marta saw her through yet another contraction then turned to Terence who'd just come in.

'She's getting very tired.'

'When did she last have pethidine?'

'An hour ago.'

'I got on to her obstetrician in Sydney. Pregnancy's been normal so far, that's something.' He knew the time had come to make a decision. 'I think we should call Dr. Ryan, would you do that?'

Marta nodded and went off to her office. Judy hovered, awaiting instructions. 'Nothing more by mouth, Sister. Get a drip up, would you? Four percent dextrose and saline.'

'Right away, doctor.' She followed Marta out.

Sandra was clearly upset and Terence moved quickly to reassure her.

'Your baby's fine. But we're not making quite as much progress as we'd like.'

'I can't keep going much longer.'

'I know. You've got what we call C.P.D., Mrs. Myers, cephalopelvic disproportion, which is an awful name for something quite simple. It means you've got a normal sized baby and a very small pelvis. So you need a Caesarean. We're going to bring an obstetrician in from Burrigan.' This news was another blow to Sandra.

'I wanted to have the baby naturally. I've been to classes ...'

'And they've stood you in good stead. But this is something outside your control.'

'Then please – can't you do it? I don't want yet another stranger!'

Her appeal opened an old wound. Terence wished he could say yes, was even, for a moment, tempted to agree.

21

But he couldn't do it.

'Dr Ryan's first rate, Mrs. Myers. There's nothing to worry about. I'll assist him. We'll get him here as soon as we can.' To Terence's consternation she started to cry again, silently. 'Are you quite sure you don't want your husband here?'

Sandra shook her head. 'I don't want anybody. Just do what you have to do.' She turned her head away. Terence caught Judy in the corridor outside, coming back to set the drip up. He murmured, 'She needs a friend, Sister Loveday.'

'Of course she does, doctor. But where's the sod of a husband? That's what I want to know.'

Tim Bourke, who'd come to see Simon after cricket practice, seemed a polite and pleasant young man, with no obvious signs of teenage moodiness. It was not he who was making the consultation difficult, it was Mrs. Bourke, who was determined not to let her son get a word in edgeways. Simon wielded his stethoscope on Tim's back and chest while he attempted pertinent questions, such as when Tim first got the headaches and what medication had been tried. Mrs. Bourke answered. They'd started four years ago when the family first moved to Wandin Valley. Tim got them every Monday. It was Dr Clarke who realised that Tim didn't like the school here and put him on the pills which really helped. Stress, you see. Simon asked Tim to describe the headaches and Mrs. Bourke did it for him: flashes of light, pain on the right side of his head, vomiting sometimes. Wasn't that right, Tim? Tim could only nod.

'And before you ask,' said Mrs. Bourke, 'there's no family history of migraine, nothing like that. We went through it all with Dr Clarke. Dr Clarke said he's basically very healthy, he's just got this thing about school. Haven't you, Tim?'

Tim looked uncomfortable and Simon thought the time had come to gently but firmly give Mrs. Bourke her marching orders. Before she knew it, he'd thanked her for her help, said he needed to see his patient on a one-to-one basis and had her out the door. Which he closed firmly behind her. Tim grinned. 'Goes on a bit, doesn't she?'

Simon smiled. 'It's called being a mother. Now – let's start again, shall we? Apart from the medication, does anything at all help to relieve the pain?'

Tim shrugged. 'Not really. Sometimes I just lie down in grandma's room for a bit. It's dark in there.'

'I see. And it only happens on Mondays?'

'Yeah. I wake up with it.'

Simon thought about that. 'You're nearly seventeen, right?' Tim nodded. 'How's life in general?'

'Not bad.'

'What do you like to do?'

'Just the usual. I've got a girlfriend, we hang out a bit. I play a lot of sport. Mainly at school, I'm in the footy and cricket teams.'

'And your studies?'

'I'm doing okay. Mrs. Jarratt, she's the year eleven co-ordinator, gives me extra lessons. You know, to help with what I miss on Mondays.'

'Tim, you don't sound to me like a kid who hates school.'

Tim looked at him with something like relief. 'That's just it. I quite like it. But they don't believe me. It's like they needed something to blame for the rotten headaches and somehow they picked on school.'

'Look. I'll write you a new prescription. But I'm not giving up, okay? There's got to be another answer.'

'Thanks,' said Tim, and it was so clearly heartfelt that Simon was encouraged, even though he hadn't a clue what the answer was. He thought that at least Tim hadn't flounced out of his surgery, hurt and upset, like Jenny Secombe.

Dairy-farming, like labour, is hard-work, the worse for going on three hundred and sixty-five days a year. Hal Secombe, Jenny's dad, was inured to it, at times even enjoyed it. He often thought about what else he might have done and rarely came up with an answer. He'd inherited the farm from his father and the rhythm of the life, the twice-a-day milking, the calving, the growing of crops to feed his herd, was in his blood. He knew better than to hope that Jenny would carry on, he wouldn't want her to. It was no life for a girl, he knew that. Besides, she had her heart set on being a teacher and that was fine by him. He just didn't want anything to shatter her dream in the meantime. Anything or anyone. Like Tony Pieri, whose panel van was just then pulling up by the gate. He unhooked the last cow from the milking machine and drove it out into the yard, watching while Jenny got out and had a last word to Tony. Then Tony drove off, without so much as a wave towards Hal. Jenny, at least, walked over to see her dad.

'Hi.'

Hal couldn't help himself. 'How come Tony never gets out of that van? Never comes in to say hello?'

'Bit shy, I think.'

'All the same – when I took a girl out, I'd go and speak to her parents. I wouldn't just sit there and blast the horn.' Jenny was embarrassed. She wanted him to think well of Tony.

'Sorry.'

Hal smiled to soften it. 'Maybe I'm just an old grump.'

Jenny didn't respond. Not like her, Hal thought. 'Hey, something up? You had a bad day?'

She shook her head.

'You're pretty late home.' It was the wrong thing to say.

'I'm sorry! I'll go and get the dinner started.' She turned abruptly and headed for the house.

'Hey, Jen! It's alright!' But she didn't stop. Hal sighed. He knew very well that it *wasn't* alright, they both knew it. They'd managed for a while after Penny died but now it just got harder everyday. A girl of fifteen needed a mother, that was it, and hard as he tried he couldn't play both roles. He wished there was someone he could talk to.

Shirley Dean was also thinking about Jenny Secombe as she finally got around to doing her shopping. Quite a dilemma the kid had given Simon – awkward for both of them, really. Shirley, who was very much a live-and-let-live sort of person, quite a free spirit in fact, thought the law, as usual, was a bit of an ass in this case and wondered what Sergeant Gilroy, he of the abundant rose garden, would think about it. Her thoughts turned to Simon and she allowed herself a small peal of laughter; she'd done her best to assist his efforts to woo her daughter, even though she knew full well it could only end in tears … She was so busy picturing the encounter, and so laden down with groceries, not to mention a wine cask, that she almost tripped over the gutter. Just as well the constabulary was there to lend a hand.

'Heaven's Shirl, nearly lost the lot there. Let me give you a hand.' And Sergeant Gilroy had taken the wine cask before she could protest.

'Silly me, head in the clouds as usual. But thank you, Frank. A pity to see Wandin Valley awash with chardonnay.'

'Like a drop of wine, do you?'

Shirley wasn't sure of the correct answer to that. 'Oh well. On occasion. The right occasion. I never drink when I'm drinking, Frank. Um – driving. It's mainly for Vicky. You know what the young ones are like. In my day it was Porphyry Pearl at Christmas. Now it's wine with everything.'

'Porphyry Pearl.' Frank smiled. 'That's going back a bit.'

'I was just a tiny tot. Here we are, thanks Frank, tremendous help, much appreciated.' She had her shopping in the back of the car in record time.

Frank wasn't letting her off that easily. 'Did you like the roses?' Shirley feigned delight.

'Oh the *roses*! Yes! So kind. So *thoughtful*.'

Frank said, with more than a little pride, 'I grew them myself.'

Shirley appeared astonished. 'Really? I don't know how you find the time. You being a policeman. And kids to look after.'

'Kids are grown up, Shirl. Left home a while ago. I'm on my own now. Can't say I like it much, either.'

Shirley could see where this was leading. 'You should get out more. Travel.'

'You do that, don't you?'

'It's the gypsy in my soul, Frank. Can't stay still for too long or I really go bonkers. Just have to bust out.'

Frank tried to imagine himself busting out and failed.

'You're what they call a citizen of the world, Shirl, aren't you? You're – sophisticated.'

Shirley sensed his loneliness and, as always, took pity.

'I wouldn't say that, Frank. I'm just restless. I really must get this stuff home.' Except that the damn car wouldn't start. She closed her eyes and tried again. Nothing. She opened her eyes, smiled at Frank, took a deep breath. Once more unto the breach. The engine started. She gave Frank a winning smile.

He called after her. 'I'll give you a ring! On the telephone!'

Shirley waved back. He wasn't sure if she'd heard him or not.

Vicky Dean was better prepared than her mother had been when a suitor appeared. Through the window of her veterinary surgery, she'd seen him arrive, dragging a reluctant canine behind him; and not just any canine but a very large English sheepdog. Vicky smelled a rat straightaway. So did Elaine Mackay, who was getting a hepatitis booster for her Jack Russell.

'Not a word, Elaine.'

Elaine grinned. 'My lips are sealed. 'Though you could do worse, Vicky. Very well-connected.'

'Huh. There you go, little fella. Does he still get up when Andy does?'

Elaine nodded. 'Three o'clock every morning, off into the bakery.'

'Nothing so loyal as a Jack Russell.'

As Elaine left she passed Simon Bowen dragging the sheepdog in through the front door. She rather liked young Dr Bowen. She sensed his frustrations with this small town only too well and understood them even better.

'Are they getting used to you yet?'

'Not really, Elaine.'

'It'll happen,' she said. 'Patience.'

'So I've been told. I hear you're trying to get the hospital a new ECG machine. Good for you.'

Elaine grinned. 'Doing my best, Simon. Patience.' They parted company and Vicky called Simon in.

'Good evening,' he said brightly, 'I think I'm the last.'

'Dr Bowen. How nice.'

Simon tried to haul the dog in behind him. 'I've got a bit of a problem with my dog. With Butch.'

'What is it?'

'He doesn't want to come in.' He pulled hard on the lead again. The dog edged into the room.

Vicky gave him the once over. 'That's your dog.' It wasn't really a question. More a statement of disbelief.

Simon already knew he was losing but he wasn't ready to give up. 'Yeah. And he wants you to come out to dinner tonight. Just the three of us.'

CHAPTER FOUR

When Vicky had stopped laughing she suggested that Butch could do with a good wash and Simon might like to help. This was not what Simon had had in mind but he could see no way out of it.

'Oh. Right.'

'You might like to borrow an apron, that's a nice suit. Italian?'

'Well. Yes.'

Vicky just smiled and lathered Butch up.

'There's something wrong with Italian suits?'

'Not at all. Very smart.'

Not what she said, Simon thought, but the way she said it. They got on with washing Butch, or rather Vicky did while Simon held him.

'So what about dinner? Just between friends?'

'I'm not sure it's such a good idea, Dr. Bowen.'

'What's this "Doctor Bowen" thing? And tell me what I have to do?'

Vicky ignored the question. 'How long have you had Butch?'

'Oh, years and years.'

'Liar.'

Simon gave up. 'Alright, yes I am. He belongs to an acquaintance.'

Vicky grinned. 'I know. Butch and I are old mates.'

Simon threw his hands in the air. 'I had to do something to get your attention!'

'Accept it. You're not my type.'

'You barely know me!'

'Poor little rich boy, isn't that you? Never took anything seriously in your life.'

'Oh, I see, a bit of class warfare. I was born with a silver spoon through no fault of my own and that's no good for a working country girl.'

'You said it.'

'It wasn't that easy, you know. Imagine having a father and a grandfather who were both famous surgeons and you can't even manage to graduate in the top ten percent! So you end up sharing a practice in some hick country town ...!'

Vicky somehow stayed calm but a distinct chill descended. 'You'd better go. I'll finish Butch off.'

Simon stalked to the door then thought better of retreat.

'No,' he said. 'You're quite wrong about me. I do think it's a hick town but that doesn't mean the people aren't nice. And it doesn't mean I don't take them seriously. I've been agonising all day about one of them. A young girl, under-age, who wants to go on the pill. I refused to give it to her, I didn't have any choice. But what if she goes out and gets pregnant?'

'There are other ways,' Vicky said.

'Oh sure. And it's not my responsibility. But it doesn't mean I don't worry. I also worry that no-one accepts me here, that they all rush to judgement on what sort of person I am, that I'm clearly not fit to work beside the great Terence Elliott!'

'You haven't been here long.'

'Four months. It'll still be the same in four years. Drop Butch back for me, would you, he doesn't like me either. Just send me the bill.' He strode to the door and was nearly through it before Vicky relented.

'Simon?'

He turned and she chucked him the towel. 'You finish Butch off and I'll get us a drink. But friends. Nothing else.'

'If that's what you want.'

'It is.' Simon gave her a grin and hid his disappointment. At least it was a start.

At the hospital, the medical staff were in a quandary which, if it weren't resolved, could soon turn into a panic. Marta had been on the phone, calling half the obstetricians in the state. The good Dr Ryan, as it happened, was operating. His partner, Dr Wilson, was on the road somewhere between his rooms and his farm and messages had been left. Their nearest colleague, Dr. Stephenson, was attending a seminar in Brisbane.

'Why did I ever leave the city?' Terence asked of no one in particular. 'So what are our options?'

'Call the air ambulance?'

Terence shook his head. 'By the time it got here – and took her to Melbourne … we'll just have to wait for Wilson to ring. Or hope that Ryan finishes quickly.'

He turned away and Marta sensed the turmoil that was going on in his head. Terence Elliott could perform a caesarean, she knew he could, but something was stopping him from doing it. She took a deep breath.

'I'm sure we'll find someone. Or Mrs Myers could lose her baby. I'll get Sister Loveday to help me prepare the theatre.'

Terence nodded. Marta stopped at the door. 'If you feel like a drink it's in the filing cabinet.'

He looked at her. She gazed blandly back. Neither mentioned that this was against hospital rules. Nor did Terence ask why she thought he might need alcohol. He knew that she understood. When she had gone he went to the cabinet and opened the drawer. Inside there was indeed a bottle of Scotch and a glass.

If Hal Secombe had been a drinking man it might have been a night to get stuck into it. But an occasional beer was as far as it went for Hal. Dinner had been a quiet, almost silent affair and now, while Jenny washed the dishes, he pretended to read an article on brucellosis in one of the farming magazines he subscribed to. The sad thing was that he loved Jenny and he sensed that right now she needed him and he should be trying to talk to her. But he wasn't very good at the deep and meaningful stuff, too often it somehow degenerated into a shouting match instead and he didn't want that to happen. So he said nothing. It was Jenny who finally took the bull by the horns. She put a cup of tea beside him and sat down.

'Can we talk for a minute, Dad?'

'Of course. What about?'

Jenny nearly didn't go on. She had a feeling this was going to be very hard indeed. Hal tried to do his bit.

'Is it something to do with school? You know, I looked at your maths book last night, I was dumbfounded. We never did stuff like that, not unless you went to uni. I don't know how you manage.'

'I like maths. I like school. It's not that.'

'Well go on.' Hal got a funny feeling then, about what was coming, that he wasn't going to like it, and he couldn't have been more right.

'It's about me and Tony.'

He got in quickly. 'Don't you think you're maybe seeing a bit too much of him? I mean, you're only fifteen, Jen, there's plenty of fish in the sea. You've still got three years of school, then teacher's college, if that's what you still want.'

'Of course it is!'

'Well then ...' He didn't know how to say it. How to tell her that she could do a great deal better for herself than Tony Pieri, that there was a big world waiting for her, full of possibilities, that patience was all she needed, the time to grow up.

'Please listen to me, Dad. Just this once, will you please listen?' She was pleading and he was surprised, he thought he had been listening.

'I'm listening.'

'And don't get angry.' Another pause. 'I love Tony ... I really love him. And he loves me.'

It took all Hal's willpower not to get angry. 'You're a child, Jenny. You don't know what love is.'

Jenny flared, it was a waste of time, she might have known it would be. 'You can patronise me all you like. You've got no idea what I think or how I feel, you haven't a clue!'

'You'd better stop seeing him, that's what I think!'

A red rag to a bull. 'No!' And she stormed off to her bedroom. Hal put his head in his hands. He never thought it would be this hard.

After twenty minutes, Jenny came back, in different clothes, carrying a handbag.

'Going somewhere?'

'Tony's taking me to the drive-in.' Right on cue, a car was heard outside and headlights flashed in the window.

Hal counted to ten. He spoke as calmly as he could. 'I'd rather you didn't go.'

'You don't trust me.'

'You're only fifteen, Jenny.'

'So you keep saying. Grandma Davis was married at fifteen!'

'Maybe I should go and talk to Tony.'

'Don't you dare!'

This defiance was something new. 'What's got into you, Jen?'

'*Me*? I'm just sick of being treated like a three year old! When I'm not doing anything wrong! Okay?' And she ran towards the door. Hal gave up then, he knew that whatever he did would only make things worse.

'You be home by eleven, Jenny! I'll be waiting up!' It sounded pathetic, he knew it did. He listened to the car door slam, heard Tony Pieri drive away with his daughter. He picked up a photo of his wife from the mantelpiece and looked at it for a long time but Penny had no answers for him either.

Molly Jones, who was young enough to remember teenage angst and who would almost certainly have sided with Jenny Secombe had she been privy to the happenings at the Secombe farm, was sitting with her husband Brendan on the banks of the Murray somewhere near Swan Hill eating fish and chips. Molly was laughing about the last anguished discussion she'd had with her mother. Caroline did not approve of this tripping off into the backblocks to live amongst heaven knows whom (probably 'white trash' in Caroline's mind) and had done her utmost to keep her daughter and son-in-law in Adelaide where standards could be maintained. She had failed and the farewells had been chilly.

'But she'll come round,' Molly said now, with more confidence than she felt.

'I hope the present's okay,' Brendan said, 'I heard an ominous tinkling sound.'

'Gosh, do you think it might have broken? Whatever it is?' She giggled. Wishful thinking. She looked at the broad reach of the river in front of them where dozens of birds were settling in for the night; swans, ducks, pelicans, ibis, making their needs known with raucous cries. The sun dipped lower. 'Isn't it beautiful? I'm glad we came the scenic route.' Brendan smiled and slipped an arm around her. He was glad they'd taken the scenic route as well, glad for a couple of quiet days alone together. He suspected there might not be too many in the weeks ahead.

The sunset was equally beautiful in Wandin Valley but Sandra Myers had no time to enjoy it. Terence checked her baby again and was reassuring, more reassuring than he felt. Marta appeared at the door with the news that Dr Ryan was finally on his way but would not be there for an hour and half. Terence moved outside to speak to her.

'We don't have an hour and a half. There are signs of foetal distress.'

Marta waited anxiously to see if Terence would do what he must.

'Is the theatre ready?'

'Yes.'

Terence nodded briskly, decision made.

'Find Simon Bowen for me, he'll have to manage the anaesthetic. Sister Dean too, we'll need her, she should be at home.'

Marta nodded. She was still concerned but Terence managed to give her a smile. 'I'm alright, Marta. It had to happen sometime.'

Marta touched his arm, a gesture of solidarity. 'You'll be fine,' she said. 'What about the husband?'

'Ring him,' Terence said. 'I'll take responsibility for that one.'

Marta went off to make the calls and Terence returned to Sandra who was in the middle of another contraction. He waited till it passed. 'We'll be taking you to theatre very soon, Mrs. Myers.'

'Are you going to do it, doctor?'

'Yes.'

'I'm glad. I know you'll do a good job.'

Terence smiled and wished he shared her confidence.

CHAPTER FIVE

In her surgery, Vicky had just opened a couple of beers. Butch was asleep, worn out by an excess of cleansing. Simon had accepted the fact that seduction was out of the question but was hoping he might at the very least be able to cut through a few of the layers of barbed wire with which Vicky so artfully surrounded herself. He asked why Vicky had chosen to return to Wandin Valley instead of practising in the city where the work for a vet was easier and the money considerably better. Vicky seemed to find it an odd question.

'I was born here,' she said. 'That's why. And my mother's here. Somebody's got to look after her.'

'She seems quite able to look after herself.'

'You think so? She can't even cook. And right now she's into pyramid healing.'

'What?'

'Sits under a pyramid and meditates.'

'I see.' He didn't.

'It removes stagnant energy and improves your aura. Or something.'

Simon had to laugh. 'Okay. She's delightfully crazy, your mum. But she still doesn't need looking after, does she? So what's the future for you?'

'The future,' said Vicky airily, 'is something I never think about.'

Simon didn't believe her. 'Everyone worries about –'

But Vicky was already talking over him.

'It's people like you, Simon, who worry about tomorrow. People with an image to live up to, all those family expectations –'

The phone was ringing and she went to answer it. Simon followed her, annoyed.

'Now hang on, that's just amateur psychology, no one ever put pressure on me!'

But Vicky was talking to Matron Kurtesz. She told Simon to shut up and passed him the phone. He took the message and hung up. 'I've got to go. Emergency.' He paused. 'You're quite wrong about me. I am not competing with my father.' He was about to leave when on impulse he grabbed Vicky and kissed her.

He got no response. He headed for the door. There he stopped and turned to look at her.

'That was clumsy. I apologise.'

'Accepted.'

Simon went. Vicky bent down and scratched Butch. Men, she thought to herself. Life would be so much simpler without them. She smiled. And alright, yes, just a little bit duller. But Simon Bowen was definitely not her type.

Shirley had been sitting under her pyramid for a good half hour when the phone rang. She had been trying her best to meditate and to ignore the heady perfume from the large bunch of roses on the coffee table. Thoughts of Frank Gilroy – and how to make him desist in his pursuit of her – kept intruding on her efforts to rid her mind and body of stagnant energy. Her aura was completely awry. And now there was the damn phone. She wanted to ignore it but couldn't. It'd be Frank, of course, begging her to go to the club, a nice steak and salad … She sighed deeply, picked up the glass of wine she'd abandoned earlier and answered the incessant ring, adopting a bright, young voice.

'Hello, Vicky Dean …'

But of course her caller was Marta Kurtesz and Shirley dropped the silly voice and was immediately businesslike. She hid her surprise when she heard that Terence was operating and promised to be at the hospital as fast as she could. She did, however, place the glass of wine on the floor in the middle of the pyramid before rushing off to change. It could be a long night and who knew how those powerful forces might improve a precocious little Shiraz?

It wasn't the healing forces of a pyramid but some modern pharmaceuticals that had made Sandra Myers feel better. Her pre-op medication had left her floating, she told Judy Loveday.

'Excellent,' said Judy, who was deftly shaving the patient. 'So you're feeling nice and relaxed then.'

'And just a bit frightened.'

Judy, who was totally on Sandra's side by now, her animosity having been directed to the absent Mr Myers, tried to offer comfort and reassurance. She wasn't very good at it but she did her best.

'Frightened? What of? You've got the best medical team in Wandin Valley, you know that? Come to think of it, the only medical team in Wandin Valley!' Sandra tried to smile. 'These caesareans – just routine.'

'So the baby will be alright?'

'Your baby will be fine. Truly. He'll be ace. He or she.' Sandra Myers was happy to stick with 'he'. She mentioned that her husband was desperate for a girl whereas she herself wanted a boy. And this time, she said with grim determination, she was getting her way. Judy asked if she had a name picked out.

'Ben. Just Ben.'

Unwisely, Judy asked, 'But what if it *is* a girl?'

Sandra turned away. 'It's not,' she said. 'It's Ben.' Judy hoped to God she was right because otherwise, she thought, there just might be trouble ahead. Like they didn't have enough already.

And Judy only knew the half of it.

In the theatre, all was in readiness. Terence, not yet scrubbed, looked around, psyching himself up for this return to a once familiar arena. The theatre itself, he thought, was better than anyone had the right to expect in a bush nursing hospital – largely due to the efforts of Elaine Mackay and her Ladies Auxiliary. That woman could get money out of a stone and he was grateful for her efforts.

Marta watched him in silence from the door. He felt her presence and turned to her. 'That bottle in your filing cabinet? It's still intact.' She just nodded but they were both relieved that he hadn't felt the need for alcohol to see him through. 'I'll go and scrub up now.'

In a few minutes the operating team were all assembled. Judy brought the humidicrib in and set about warming it; Simon prepared for the anaesthetic. Shirley, who along with Judy was scouting, asked casually, 'Can someone fill me in?'

Marta explained that they'd be performing a routine caesarean section for emergency reasons. The baby was four weeks early and the patient was C.P.D.

Judy added, unnecessarily, that she was also loaded with money and desperate to have a boy.

'She'll have to take what comes, won't she?' said Shirley.

'I guess,' Judy said. 'But she's pretty uptight. Something to do with the husband. Who should be here but isn't. Probably off somewhere counting their millions.' While she was laughing immoderately at this little sally, Terence returned, scrubbed up.

'Right. I'd appreciate it if we kept the noise to a minimum, please.'

Judy couldn't help herself. 'All quiet on the set, thanks.' Terence looked at Marta who looked heavenwards.

'Bring Mrs. Myers in now, please Judy.' Judy scurried out. Terence shook his head. 'I know, I know,' Marta said quickly. 'But she's a very good nurse.'

'I hope so,' was all Terence said and tried to hide his nervousness. Simon exchanged a brief glance with Shirley but both refrained from commenting on the elephant in the room – did Terence Elliott have a clue what he was doing? Only Marta Kurtesz looked unperturbed.

The crew of the spacecraft *Nostromo* had plenty to be perturbed about but few at the Burrigan Drive-In seemed much concerned with their fate. Attention was drawn away from the screen by any number of distractions: hamburgers, hot chips, tinnies, soft drinks, whingeing kids in the back seat and raging hormones. Tony Pieri's panel van appeared, at first glance, to be empty but its occupants had merely moved to the mattress in the back section and were indulging in some pretty heavy necking.

It was good at first, it always was ... while Tony kissed her and fondled her breasts, Jenny let herself get carried away on a girlish dream of love everlasting. But when he became more insistent, when he pressed himself against her, started to force her legs apart, then everything changed. Then her mother's face loomed large and unwanted admonitions about keeping herself nice rang in her ears. There was a story she'd read not so long ago, in a magazine, about a home for unmarried mothers, and she had a sudden image of herself being dragged out of school and sent off there. She pushed Tony away.

'What's up?'

'That's enough.'

'Oh come, Jen! You can't get me all worked up and just stop!' He tried to get her back in the mood, he kissed her again, pulled her close, slid his hand inside the leg of her panties.

'I said no, Tony!' And suddenly she was straightening her clothes, climbing back to the front seat of the van. Tony was angry. After a while he clambered into the front beside her. She stared at the screen, tears sliding down her cheeks.

'You're angry.'

'You bet I am.'

'I'm sorry.'

'Sorry?!'

'I don't know what to do …' The tears flowed, unchecked. Tony was exasperated.

'I thought you wanted it.'

'I did. It's just – I'm scared.' Tony didn't get it. Jenny wasn't normally a weepy sort of girl, he didn't know how to handle this at all. Had he been more sensitive, he might have realised that a little tenderness and sympathy could have won her over – but he was way too young to understand that.

'I wouldn't hurt you.'

'It's not that.'

'What then? You worried about getting pregnant?'

'Of course I am! And there's Mum …'

'Your *mum?* Jen, she's dead, what's she got to do with it?'

Jenny suddenly realised the impossibility of trying to explain. She'd been twelve when Penny died. They'd had time to share some precious mother/daughter moments, to talk of Jenny's approaching maturity, of love, and sex. Her mother had said, if it makes you feel dirty or guilty, Jenny, then don't do it, because that's not what it's about. The words had stuck and somehow the back of the panel van always brought them back. It wasn't Tony's fault, she loved him, of course she did … oh why was it all so complicated! The tears flowed again.

Tony wanted to shake her. But he wasn't a bad kid. He slid an arm around her shoulders and patted her awkwardly and wondered why girls were so uptight about everything.

If Terence Elliott was feeling the strain he certainly wasn't showing it. In the operating theatre, Sandra Myers was draped, anaesthetised and ready for her caesarian section. Terence painted her belly with antiseptic, put the gauze and forceps down on the dirty trolley next to Shirley Dean and calmly called for the scalpel. Marta passed it to him. He put several light scratches on Sandra's belly. These would assist with alignment when the suturing was done after the operation. He paused for a moment. And then he made an unexpected statement.

'I'm going to do a Pfannenstiel incision,' he said. No one said a word. They didn't need to. The shock was palpable. The Pfannenstiel or bikini line incision was not one that would normally be attempted by a country GP. Simon and Shirley did their best to hide their astonishment. Marta remained calm, watching with interest. Terence's hand moved swiftly, deftly and the job was done. He asked for forceps and curved scissors and these were handed to him. Simon checked Sandra's blood pressure. She was doing well. Terence kept up a casual commentary, announcing that the peritoneum was exposed.

Once again, Simon and Shirley exchanged a glance. Terence's expertise was proving an eye-opener for both of them. Simon, in particular, had a dozen unspoken questions. He wasn't sure if, or when, they might be answered.

CHAPTER SIX

'Retractors.' Terence was preparing for the uterine incision. Sandra Myers' baby was a step closer to entering the world. It crossed Marta's mind that after Sandra's desperate flight from whatever it was that had so troubled her, a good outcome was at last in sight. What a pity they hadn't been able to reach the husband. The soon-to-be-father. Even if she didn't want him, Marta was inclined to agree with Terence – he had a right to see his child. Terence called for a scalpel, Simon checked the patient's blood pressure and pulse rate and Terence, more relaxed now, proceeded.

In quite a short time, the baby's head was free. Simon saw that Sandra's pulse rate, however, was increasing. She was given extra fluids, plasma expander, ergotamine. And then came the moment that no doctor, no nurse, ever tires of. Terence delivered the baby from Sandra's uterus.

'A little girl,' he said. 'And quite a good size considering she's four weeks early.'

'But she wanted a boy!' Judy said.

Terence was not amused. 'If the baby's healthy, sister, then Mrs Myers will have to be satisfied. We can hardly put her back.'

The cord was cut and the baby was handed to a slightly abashed Judy. Soon after it cried lustily. Terence and Simon at last exchanged a long look. Simon gave Terence a tiny nod, an acknowledgement of a job well done. Terence smiled. 'Let's close up,' he said. Marta handed him forceps and catgut. She alone knew what an ordeal it had been for him, this seemingly simple operation which he had performed with such flair.

Sigourney Weaver's ordeal with the Alien was also over. She had put herself into stasis in her lonely space shuttle where she would remain for the next fifty-seven years.

'Stupid film,' Tony said as the credits rolled.

Jenny said nothing, just got out and replaced the speaker on its hook. It was actually a pretty good film and they both knew it. They joined the line of cars edging out of the drive-in. The night had been a disaster and Jenny blamed herself; first the row with her dad, then Tony, she couldn't get anything right. He drove her home faster than he should have.

Hal Secombe, sitting up pretending to do some accounts, was relieved to hear the van pull up; for once, he was also relieved when it left almost immediately. He wasn't in the mood for pleasantries with Tony Pieri. He took a deep breath: please God, could he and Jenny not have a fight? She came in. 'Hello. How was the film?'

'Good, yeah. Bit scary.'

'Want to put the kettle on?'

'Righto.' Both of them trying so hard.

'Hey, I meant to tell you. The Davidson place – there's people moving in. Saw Bob Hatfield there today, reckons the agent sent him to look at the generator.'

'It's a dump, that place. Needs a heap of work.'

'I guess they know what they're in for.'

Jenny went on making the tea. Eventually she brought it to the table in the blue and white cups her mother had always loved. Jenny only had to think about those cups and she wanted to cry, which was silly but she couldn't help it. She sat down and traced a finger around the cornflowers on the saucer. 'Can we talk, Dad?'

'Sure.'

'I want to ask you something.'

'Go on. I'm listening.'

'I know you don't believe me when I say I love Tony. But it's true. I do love him. And he loves me. And we want to get married.'

Hal's sugar spoon clattered on to the table.

'*Married*?'

'Oh, not right away! No. Not until he's twenty-one. I'll be eighteen then.'

'Oh. I see. Plenty of time to think about it.'

'Plenty of time to change my mind. That's what you're thinking. But I won't.' She paused for a moment. 'And that's why I want to go on the pill.' For a minute it didn't register with Hal. 'The contraceptive pill, Dad. And the doctor says I need your permission.'

It registered then alright. Hal got it loud and clear. And any thought of staying calm and rational went out the window. He wondered if Jenny had totally lost her mind. Did she honestly expect to get his *permission* to shack up with Tony Pieri? To make out with him in that sin bin? What on earth would her mother think? Well thank God she wasn't around to hear it!

At the end of it Hal was shouting and Jenny was in tears for the third time that night; in tears with her hands over her ears. Poor girl; her stars were veering wildly off course and you did not have to believe in astrology to know that it was only going to get worse. At fifteen, that is what generally happened.

They sat there for a long time, Jenny and Hal, while the tea got cold, both of them feeling wretched. Finally, Hal spoke.

'Jen. I'm really sorry I shouted. But this's all come as a bit of a shock. What do you say we sleep on it. Have a talk in the morning.'

Jenny just nodded. It was all too hard. For both of them.

Before long, Sandra Myers would also have some hard decisions to make but it was too soon, even Judy Loveday could see that. She decided not to mention the errant husband and father yet again.

'Hi there, how are you feeling? Any pain?'

Sandra shook her head.

'Anaesthetic's still doing its stuff. You might be a bit sore later on.'

'Where is he, where's my baby?'

'One thing you'll have to get used to, he's a she, Mrs. Myers. You've got a lovely little girl.'

'What?'

'We've popped her in a humidicrib. You know, being four weeks prem. But she's doing fine, a really great Apgar. And absolutely gorgeous!'

'Unbelievable,' Sandra said bitterly.

'Sorry?'

'He got what he wanted. He always does.' She started to cry again, leaving Judy, for once, at a loss.

'You'll feel better tomorrow. When you get to see her. Such a beautiful little thing –'

'I don't want to see her! Not tomorrow. Not ever. Please … just leave me alone. And she turned her face to the wall.

Judy, who adored all babies and sometimes despaired that she might never have any of her own, felt totally inadequate to handle the situation and went to Marta's office for advice. Simon found them both there a few minutes later.

'Terence gone already?'

'Yes,' Marta said, 'he seemed in a hurry to get home.'

Simon was disappointed; he'd been hoping Terence might have suggested a drink. But he just said, lightly, 'It was a great job he did.'

Marta smiled. 'I think we're all agreed on that. But Judy's worried that Mrs Myers seems to be rejecting the baby.'

'Oh surely not. She's perfect!'

'She's a girl,' said Judy. 'Just what her blasted husband wanted. Oh well. Maybe she'll change her mind in the morning.' She said her goodbyes and went off home.

'I wish I could find the blasted husband,' Marta sighed. 'I've left enough messages for him.'

Simon thought the man would probably turn up when he was good and ready. His own curiosity on another matter entirely was getting the better of him. 'Tell me something, Marta. Have you ever seen Terence operate before?'

Marta pretended to be busy with some filing. 'No, I haven't.'

'And yet you didn't seem at all surprised. This man – who's supposed to be a country GP – does a Pfannenstiel incision … in five minutes he's at the peritoneum … where did he get that good, I wonder?'

'You'll have to ask him.'

'You mean, you know but you're not saying.'

'I'm tired, Simon. Time I went home. I want to ride early in the morning, I missed out today. You did well yourself this evening, we made a good team.' She picked up her bag but before she headed for the door she stopped to say one more thing.

'When you do ask Terence questions – and I know

you will – just bear in mind that he operated tonight because circumstances demanded it. He didn't find it easy. And I don't know if or when he will do it again. I listened once when he needed to talk and I'm not even sure that I know all his story. Gently, Simon. Go gently.'

She left then and Simon felt he'd come very close to putting his rather large foot right in it. So he did not go, uninvited, to Terence's flat (which was just as well) but instead took himself home to the rather boring little unit attached to the Wandin Valley Hotel/Motel where he was currently living.

It was not, Simon thought as he opened the door, that he couldn't afford something a little better. It was sheer laziness. He'd booked in when he first came to town and hadn't got around to moving. This, at least, was what he told himself. The truth was a little more complicated.

Simon was not on a salary, he had actually – with the help of his parents – bought into the practice, so his financial stake in the town was considerable. But this was a fact he did not like to dwell on. He did not want to feel tied to this rural backwater; the idea that he might remain here for ten or fifteen years had little appeal. The events of the evening had been interesting and also unsettling; he knew that no doctor could gain the skills displayed by Terence Elliott in a place like Wandin Valley. So where had he got them and why had he left? And why was Simon himself not acquiring similar expertise? He poured himself a glass of wine – and he almost never drank alone – and sat there pondering these and other questions and feeling deeply discontented. Feeling, in fact, that he had probably made a huge mistake coming to Wandin Valley in the first place. Only the challenge posed by Vicky Dean made the thought of any extended stay bearable.

He should have talked it over with Frank Gilroy who, driving home after dealing with a minor domestic, was contemplating the challenge posed by Vicky's mother. Clearly it was going to take more than roses to win the redoubtable Shirley Dean and indeed Frank sometimes wondered whether, if he should ever succeed, he might not live to rue the day. He admired Shirley enormously, she was everything he himself was not: a sophisticated woman of the world, witty and clever and bright, a woman who in Frank's eyes sparkled like diamonds. But he knew she had a very sharp tongue and he was afraid she might some time turn it on him, might see him as just a bumbling country cop. Shirley, who was the kindest of souls could also, he was pretty sure, be devastatingly cruel. But he was a brave man and willing to take the risk – if he ever got the chance.

Of the women at the centre of all this soul-searching, one had helped to bring new life into the world and had therefore passed, on the whole, a most satisfactory evening. Not so her daughter. Vicky, who was a very good vet but a lousy businesswoman, had stayed at the surgery after Simon left, sorting through myriad bits of paper, trying to work out who owed her what and getting nowhere. She had a fridge full of eggs and cream and home-made butter and a cupboard packed with jams and pickles but her cash-flow was nothing like it should have been. She realised she would have to take steps. And would if she knew what steps to take. Like much else in Wandin Valley that night, it got shunted into the too-hard basket.

Vicky arrived home to find her mother retrieving a glass of wine from under the pyramid. Words were unnecessary, Vicky's look said it all. She confined herself to pleasantries.

'Everything alright at the hospital?'

'Emergency caesar. A dear little girl. Mother and baby both doing well.'

'Excellent.' Vicky watched while Shirley sipped the

wine, rolling it around her mouth as if it were, at the very least, a first growth Bordeaux. 'Um …?'

Shirley swallowed and smiled. 'Aged ten years.'

Vicky started to laugh. 'You or the wine?'

'Don't be rude to your mother. The pyramid has definitely made a difference.'

Vicky could hardly contain her mirth. 'If you say so, Mum. Though how an aluminium pyramid can turn Chateau Cardboard into Grange Hermitage …'

'Did I mention Grange? I merely said it had made a difference. See for yourself.' Shirley proffered the glass which Vicky ignored. 'No thanks, I'll make some coffee.'

She headed into the kitchen. Shirley flopped into a chair with her wine. 'One thing I learnt tonight – Terence Elliott is a very good surgeon.'

'I imagine he's good at most things,' Vicky said.

'Oh not you too,' Shirley said. 'I don't want you joining up.'

'*What?*'

'The Terence Elliott Fan Club. It's oversubscribed. Besides, I thought you liked Simon Bowen.'

'I prefer older men,' Vicky said, just to be annoying. 'And besides, it's Simon who's interested in me.'

'Yes, strange that,' said Shirley. 'Most odd.'

'Well thank you, mother dear!'

'No really, he's Aries, you're Capricorn. Nothing in common at all. Except that you're both young and reasonably intelligent. Maybe it's a case of opposites attracting.'

'I've told you! I am *not* attracted!' She brought her coffee and put it down on the table, noticing the roses for the first time. 'Nice roses.' She pulled the card out and peered at it, curious. 'Warm regards, Frank. Frank Gilroy?'

Shirley shrugged. Vicky grinned broadly. 'Sergeant

Frank Gilroy, widower of this parish and Sister Shirley Dean, amateur pyramidologist. Oh boy, talk about opposites!'

Shirley affected boredom. 'Oh do stop it, Vicky. He's like a schoolboy with a crush – and believe me, it won't last. I'll make damn sure it doesn't.'

Vicky was not to be deterred. 'I don't know, Mum ... when you think about it, what could be more suitable? He's the right age ... impeccable character ... very fit, you know he jogs every morning? I'd get right back under that pyramid if I were you, start conserving some energy!'

Shirley gave her daughter a look that was far from motherly and rose to her feet. 'I think I'll have a long, hot bath,' she said. 'I might stay there for hours. If the phone rings, I'm unavailable.'

Terence Elliott was another who was unavailable. Had his phone rung it's unlikely he would have even heard it. Terence could barely remember driving home from the hospital, even though he was stone cold sober. He did not stay that way for long. Once inside his flat above the clinic, with the door closed firmly behind him, he poured himself a very large single malt whisky. He needed something to stop the memories which were threatening to overwhelm him; something to stop his hands, so calm and steady an hour ago, from trembling uncontrollably. It took a while but gradually the whisky did its job. No wonder the Scots called it *uisge beatha,* or 'water of life'.

CHAPTER SEVEN

The sun rose, bringing new hope to several of Wandin Valley's residents and continuing despair to others. Away to the west, on the banks of the Murray just upstream from Swan Hill, Brendan and Molly Jones embraced hope after a short struggle. They had booked into a camping ground for the night and had stayed in a grandly named 'chalet', a one-room bunkhouse whose mod cons included a bathroom of sorts, a two-burner stove and quite the most hideous lino either had ever encountered. They sat outside now on two plastic chairs which constituted the 'barbecue area', drinking tea, listening to the dawn chorus and feeling pretty much at peace with the world. Well, Brendan was.

'Didn't the agent say there was lino in the kitchen, Brendan?' Molly was thinking forward to their new house.

'I think he might have.'

'Well whatever the pattern, it couldn't be worse than that one, could it?' She nodded towards the chalet. 'I'm taking comfort from that.'

Brendan grinned but Molly went on in more serious vein than he'd expected. 'I suppose we were totally mad, weren't we? Buying the place sight unseen.'

'Not *exactly* sight unseen. We got a brochure, remember? And two maps. And half a dozen extra photos.'

'Not the same as walking through it though, is it? Getting a real feel for it. I mean, what if it's a terrible dump?'

Brendan leant forward, took her cup out of her hands and held them tightly. 'Molly, we *know* it's a terrible dump. That's why we could afford it. Surely you're not getting cold feet? Now that we're only a day away?'

'No! No, I'm not. Honestly.'

'Darling, it's going to be fine –'

'Of course it is. I just had a moment of panic, that's all. Lying in bed last night, with the moonlight on that awful lino, I got to wondering how bad the house really is. You know how your mind plays games at three o'clock in the morning ...'

Brendan, who'd had a few moments of panic himself, pulled her close.

'Even if it's a pigsty, we'll turn it into a palace, Molly Jones. I promise you.'

But Molly shook her head. 'No, you've got to earn a living. *I'll* turn it into a palace.' She smiled at him. 'We do actually have a pigsty, remember. Not to mention a pig.'

'Ah yes, what's her name? Dorothy?'

'Doris.'

'Can't wait to meet her. I've been reading up on how to make salami.' He ducked out of Molly's clutches and backed quickly away.

In another, smaller river – a tributary of the Murray, as it happened – Terence Elliott was clearing his head with a morning swim. It was a deep and quiet waterhole; few people ever went there, even in the height of summer and especially not this early in the day. Terence crossed it a couple of times doing a lazy crawl, keeping an eye out for snakes and fallen trees and finding neither, then turning to float on his back and gaze at the clear summer sky. Not a cloud to be seen; the district needed rain but it would not be coming today. He got the sense that he was being watched and flipped over to tread water. On the bank, smiling at him from the back of a bay gelding called The General, was Marta Kurtesz.

'Good morning, Dr Elliott!'

'Matron. You crept up on me!' He swam closer to the bank.

'Is the water nice?'

'Come in and see.'

'I wish I'd brought my bathers.'

Terence raised an eyebrow.

Marta ignored the implication. 'Do you swim here often?'

'I do, yes. It's a great spot.'

'Then I might join you another time.' And she gave him a grin, dug her heels into The General and cantered off. Terence watched her go. And thought, not for the first time, how much he admired her.

Judy Loveday pulled the curtain back in Sandra Myers' room at Wandin Valley Hospital. Sunlight flooded in but no laughter accompanied it. Judy carried a small bunch of flowers which she'd already put into a vase.

'Good morning, how are we? Flowers for you, I stole them myself from next door's garden. They're away so what they don't know won't hurt them.' She put the vase on a shelf provided for the purpose. 'How did you sleep?'

'Hardly at all. I was in pain, I still am!'

'Well that's to be expected, I'm sure the night nurse gave you something. I bet your tummy's sore too, can I just have a bit of a look-see?' She checked Sandra's wound and did the usual obs; everything was fine. 'You're doing very well, Mrs. Myers. And so's your baby. Like I told you – she's totally gorgeous. And a very good size –'

'I don't want to know, alright? I don't want to hear about the baby! Will you please not talk about her and just get me something for the pain!'

Judy gave up once again on Mrs Myers and went to get the analgesia Terence had prescribed, announcing to Marta that she was starting to wonder if maybe Mrs Myers wasn't just a bit of a spoilt brat after all – though of course you never knew what her sod of a husband had put her through. Marta decided to deliver the medication herself and found Sandra in tears yet again. She hoped the absent Mr Myers was responsible for at least some of this sadness; that might prove easier to deal with than post-natal depression, which was looming as a distinct possibility.

'I never realised that having a baby would hurt so much.'

'It's not the baby, Mrs. Myers. It's the fact that you've had surgery. But you'll heal very quickly, I promise you, by tomorrow you'll start feeling quite a lot better. Dr Elliott will come to see you later … he did a wonderful job, by the way, you'll be able to wear a bikini again next summer.'

Sandra seemed unimpressed.

Marta spoke gently but firmly. 'Mrs Myers. Just down the hall in a humidicrib is a baby girl. Your little girl. Wouldn't you like to say hello?'

'Don't you understand? I don't want her. I don't want anything to do with her!'

Marta thought that Sandra couldn't make it much

plainer than that. And yet something didn't sit right about this whole situation. They needed to get to the bottom of it fast. For one thing, that baby would soon be very hungry.

Still in her pyjamas, Shirley Dean was sitting under her pyramid. She liked to think that its cosmic vibrational energy cleared her mind for the day ahead. At the very least, she found it relaxing. So relaxing that she managed to ignore the insistent ringing of the telephone. Vicky the unbeliever, dragged unwillingly from bed, was not pleased.

'Couldn't you have answered it?'

'It's him. No one else'd ring at this hour.' Vicky gritted her teeth and answered the phone. It was indeed Sergeant Frank Gilroy. Vicky gushed.

'Not at all, Sergeant, we've been up for hours! Hang on, I'll see if I can find Mum.' Shirley shook her head violently, indicating that she was not to be found. Vicky put her hand over the mouthpiece and hissed, 'He's a nice man. Talk to him!' Shirley closed her eyes and sought inner peace.

'Sorry, Sergeant,' Vicky said to the waiting Frank. 'Mum's sitting under a pyramid meditating. I'll get her to call you back when she's in harmony with the universe.'

She hung up. Shirley glared. 'You could have told him I was in the shower.'

'I think he should have to get to know the real you.'

'Why? It's not like I'd ever marry a policeman.'

'Then tell him. Do the decent thing.'

Vicky headed for the bathroom. Shirley yelled after her.

'I'm too scared. Have you ever heard of police brutality?'

Vicky laughed. 'He grows roses, Mum. What's he

going to do? Hit you over the head with a bunch of floribundas?'

Later, over breakfast, Vicky tackled the subject again, trying to extract a promise that Shirley would indeed return the good sergeant's call. Shirley could see no reason why she should. Vicky repeated that Frank deserved to know where he stood. 'Or perhaps, Mum, you're not so sure after all where *you* stand?'

'Meaning?'

'Perhaps, deep down, you *harbour feelings*?' Vicky ducked in time to miss the jam spoon. 'Gosh,' she said, 'Is that the time? I must dash. I'm due at Hal Secombe's place in twenty minutes, got to vaccinate his calves. Don't do anything I wouldn't do, please, Mum?'

CHAPTER EIGHT

Vicky was still grinning to herself driving out to Hal Secombe's a short time later. She adored her mad mother and she could see why someone like Frank Gilroy might find her attractive but the thought of Frank as a future step-father was a little hard to get her head around. She waved to Jenny Secombe waiting for the school bus and got a little half-wave back; Jenny, Vicky thought, must have a maths exam or something, she did not look happy. Nor did her father when Vicky found him with the calves already yarded down behind the milking shed. Vicky liked Hal, most of the town did. He was admired for getting on with things after his wife died of breast cancer; that's what country people did, got on with it. Private misfortune did not stop you from running the farm, from doing a good job of bringing up your daughter or from pitching in when someone else needed a hand. Hal got full marks in all areas and few in Wandin Valley would have backed his daughter's current harsh assessment of him.

Hal and Vicky worked together smoothly, they'd done

this sort of thing before. He dragged the calves out of the pen and pushed them down the chute while she used an automatic vaccinating gun to protect them against brucellosis. When the job was complete, Vicky queried Hal's sombre mood. She thought perhaps it might be the weather, everyone was getting worried about the lack of rain, but he said he still had plenty of feed. He managed a faint smile. 'I don't suppose you've got time for a cuppa? I could do with a woman's advice.'

In no rush on this fine morning, Vicky agreed. They sat on the verandah, shaded by the enormous old wisteria, and Hal let it all spill out, the whole sorry saga of teenage passion which was currently causing such anguish in the Secombe household. Vicky listened quietly and thought it would really all be quite funny unless you were actually forced to live it and then it would be hell.

'I know the Pieris. Good Catholic family. If Tony's putting the hard word on Jenny, his mother had better not hear about it.' She smiled then, trying to lighten the mood, to let Hal see it wasn't the end of the world. 'I was fourteen when I first fell in love.'

'Who was the lucky fellow?'

'Bob Dennis. It lasted a whole month. If only I could have seen the future – he's got three pubs now.'

Hal almost smiled. 'The problem with Jenny – she thinks it's going to last forever. Her and Tony. And because of that ... well. I told you.' And he didn't want to repeat it.

Vicky, however, had no such qualms. 'She wants to go on the pill.'

Hal nodded. 'It's like she's asking me to say it's okay, Vicky. To – sanction it, you know? And I can't do that!'

'You talked about it?'

'Not really. We shouted a lot. We were going to talk this morning but she left the house without a word. I just don't know where to go from here.'

'Are they actually having sex, Hal?'

'I don't think so. No – I'm sure they're not. From what she's said, it's like going on the pill – with my blessing – would make it okay.'

'Like it wouldn't feel wrong any more?'

'Yes.'

Vicky sighed. 'Oh dear. Who'd be fifteen again?'

'So what do I say to her? Any ideas?'

Vicky wanted to say, Hal, she'll get over it, it will be alright, she's a sensible kid. But she felt that would be taking the easy way out. And what if it didn't turn out alright but ended up like that movie, what was it called? Shirley made her watch it on TV; Alan Bates, *A Kind Of Loving,* that was it, two young lives more or less ruined when the girl got pregnant. That was no solution.

She finally said, 'We both know that laying down the law's not going to work.'

'Like a red rag to a bull,' Hal said.

'And you can't forbid her to see him. Lots of wide open spaces out there.'

'So?'

'I think you've got to be honest. Tell Jenny exactly how you feel. That you love her and you don't want to see her get hurt. Ask her at the very least to wait until she's sixteen.'

'And if she won't agree?'

'Then there's not a lot you can do. Not unless you want to risk losing her.'

Hal stared into his cup. 'Bit of a shock, finding your little girl has suddenly grown up.'

Vicky got up. 'She's not there yet, Hal. She still needs her dad. I'd better go, before brucellosis sweeps the country.'

Hal got up to. 'Thanks, Vicky. It's been a help just having someone to talk to.'

'Any time. My pleasure.'

He walked with her to her car. 'I hear there's a good show at the club on Saturday night. I don't suppose you'd like to come with me? A sort of thank you for the counselling session.' He sensed her hesitation. 'I haven't been out a lot since Penny died. Maybe it's time I learnt to make conversation again.'

Vicky suddenly thought, why not? 'That sounds nice, Hal. I haven't been to the club for quite a while.'

He smiled, pleased.

At the hospital, nothing had happened to brighten the mood of Sandra Myers and the staff were becoming concerned about both mother and child. From the nursery, where she was playing with the baby's tiny fingers, Judy Loveday could just hear Terence and Marta talking about it.

'I suppose there's no chance she'll want to breast feed, not in her current state of mind.'

'Terence, she won't even *see* the child! So we've been asking around – and a couple of new mums in town have agreed to donate some milk.'

'Well at least the baby won't starve.'

'It's such a rare thing around here, an unwanted child. Well, except when the mother isn't married, perhaps ...'

Terence grinned. 'I wouldn't class that as rare, exactly.'

He wondered whether they ought to keep on trying to find the husband. They both agreed it was difficult; they had no idea how things really stood between Sandra Myers and the father of her child, whether what had occurred had been a lovers' quarrel or something much more serious, even a case of domestic violence. But if the situation were not resolved and they remained apart and if Sandra continued her outright rejection of the baby, then the father might be the child's only option.

'That little girl is going to need one of them, Marta. Isn't she?'

Marta said, 'I'll keep trying to find him then. But unless we contact the police, I'm not sure how much more I can do.'

'Let's hope it doesn't come to that. I've got a house call to make, old Miss Bird, I might be sending her into you if her pleurisy's no better.'

'I shall pray for a miracle cure,' said Marta. 'I can do without Miss Bird at the moment.'

Terence grinned. 'She's a dear old thing.'

'I'm sure she was a wonder droving cattle on the outer Barcoo or wherever it was. In my hospital she's a pest, Terence. No other word for it.'

Terence was not without sympathy. They had all heard Miss Bird's stories of her droving days – probably once too often. He left on his mission of mercy and Marta tried once more to track down the errant Mr Myers – since they'd left messages all over Sydney but he was clearly never in one place for more than five minutes.

Shirley Dean was also searching for that which was lost – in her case, thirty dollars missing from petty cash. Unlike Bernie Myers, it only had a cash book and a small tin to hide in but it was doing an equally good disappearing act. Simon, unaware of the problem, had stopped to admire the latest offering from Frank's garden.

'Another gentle reminder of Sergeant Gilroy's devotion?' Shirley chose to ignore him.

'Thirty dollars. Where on earth can it be …?'

'I bet the poor man gets about as much encouragement as I do but does he give up? Never!'

'It must have been used for something …'

'What comes next, I wonder? A midnight serenade

beneath your window?'

'Oh please God, no.' She looked at Simon. 'The whole town's talking about it. And I don't know how to stop him.'

'Why bother? Why not just enjoy it? And by the way – I took the thirty dollars. Demand it back from your daughter.'

'Vicky?'

'It's what she charges for a dog wash!'

He was about to say exactly what he thought of that when Frank Gilroy came in and he quickly disappeared into his consulting room. He was careful, however, to leave the door ajar.

Frank greeted Shirley in a serious tone. He'd come, he said, about her car. Shirley, of course, immediately thought the worst.

'My car? What have I done?'

'Done, Shirl? Nothing that I know of, do you have a guilty conscience?'

'No! Not at all.'

'Good. Though you should have. Letting rust get into the door like that. Rust is corrosion, as I'm sure you know. Leave it and you'll end up with nothing but a pile of flakes.' He rubbed his fingers together to demonstrate what would be left of Shirley's car.

'That bad?'

'That bad.'

'Um – so what should I do?'

'You? Nothing. I'll fix it for you tomorrow. Will you be home tomorrow? Say around five? That's what I rang about.'

'You rang?'

'Didn't Vicky tell you?'

There was nothing for it but to lie through her teeth. 'No. She didn't. Not a word. Hopeless in the mornings, Vicky, so vague!'

'Never mind. You did like the roses?'

'The roses! Oh, beautiful!'

'Grew them myself.'

'Yes, yes you told me.' She saw a life-raft in the form of Simon hovering at his door. 'Oh, coming, doctor, right away. Sorry, Frank, I'll have to go but thank you! For the rust – and the roses!'

'No worries, Shirl. See you tomorrow, then.' Sergeant Gilroy left, feeling that had all gone quite well.

Shirley shut Simon's door firmly behind her. 'You heard all that?' Simon admitted that he had. 'He makes me feel like a criminal. The minute I see him, I wonder what I've done wrong.'

'When all he wanted was to save you from a bit of rust.'

'So romantic.'

'Well it is, in a way,' said Simon. 'Caring, at the very least.' Shirley rolled her eyes. 'You know, all things considered, you could do a lot worse, Shirl. Why don't you give him a go?'

Shirley was quiet for a moment, remembering Jack Dean and twenty-odd years of regret. She looked at Simon and shook her head. 'I tried that once, way, way back. Giving someone a go. Didn't work then and I can't see it working now.' She smiled, lightening the moment. 'Frank's not my type, darling. He jogs at five in the morning. He a fanatic about his roses. And then he's a cop! What if I wanted to do something a tiny bit illegal?'

Simon grinned. 'Surely not.'

'I like to keep my options open. No, Frank will make someone a wonderful husband but it won't be me.' Simon let it rest.

Terence arrived a few minutes later and went over the morning's list with Shirley. It wasn't too bad – but if it turned out that he was needed at the hospital again, then Wandin Valley's sick would have to make do with

Simon, however they felt about young doctors fresh from the big smoke. 'I've just sent Norah Bird off in an ambulance by the way,' Terence said. 'So she won't be coming in, she's Marta's problem.'

'Poor darling,' said Shirley.

'Which one?'

'Marta!' Shirley laughed. 'Though I can't help having a soft spot for Birdie.'

'I know, we all do.' He hummed a few bars of *The Queensland Drover* and went off into Simon's room. Simon removed his feet from his desk.

'Good morning.'

'It is indeed,' Terence said. 'Done any tropical medicine?'

'Some. Not a lot.'

'I've got a patient coming in later, just back from Fiji. He's got what I thought was just a bad case of TD – diarrhoea, bloating, nausea, cramps but it's not getting any better and none of the usual stuff has helped.'

'I've got some notes somewhere …' Simon started to rummage in his bookcase. 'They seem to be recommending a megadose nowadays. Should knock it off in forty-eight hours.' While he went on searching Terence got round to the real reason for his visit.

'You were a great help last night, Simon. Couldn't have managed without you.'

'I didn't notice you needing much assistance, mate, I can't remember when I saw such a professional job.'

'Thanks.'

Simon pretended to still be looking for the notes. 'I guess you specialised before you came here, then.'

'That's right.' But he didn't enlarge on the subject and Simon, remembering Marta's admonition to go gently, did not ask any more questions.

'Here we are, found them.' He smiled and handed the notes to Terence.

'Thanks, I'll make sure you get them back. Can you hold the fort here if I'm needed again at the hospital?'

'Sure. Is that likely?'

'I honestly don't know. Sandra Myers is physically fine. But her mental state is another thing altogether. And then there's Miss Bird, of course.' They both allowed themselves a smile.

CHAPTER NINE

Miss Bird was as sharp as a tack for all of her seventy plus years, but her body was failing her and that was a source of constant frustration. She waged a constant war against the lupus which she'd now had for over twenty years, and its many side effects, such as this current bout of pleurisy. She was still trying to run the family farm with her widowed brother and felt she should be there now, not lying in the hospital bed which Marta and Judy Loveday were trying to get her to occupy. Even Marta was losing patience.

'Really, Miss Bird, if you won't co-operate, I'll have to get Dr Elliott to come and knock you out with something.'

'You wouldn't.'

'Try me. This pleurisy is serious. Or he wouldn't have sent you in.'

Judy chipped in. 'You do want to recover, don't you? Otherwise, you'll never get home.' Brutal but effectual, Marta thought, because Miss Bird looked chastened and suddenly allowed them to help her into bed. She was a small woman, thin and wiry, and for once she looked vulnerable.

'I have to get better. Bruce can't manage on his own.'

Marta smiled at her. 'Just do as we ask then.' A phone was ringing. 'I'll leave you with Sister Loveday.'

Miss Bird smiled at her captive. 'Why don't you sit down? We can have a nice chat. Did I ever tell you about the time Bruce and I drove twelve hundred sheep from Tibooburra to Cobar? I was just a slip of a girl then, younger than you.'

'I believe you did tell me, Miss Bird. You have a rest now, I'll be back when I've seen to my other patients, okay?' She fled, with Miss Bird's plaintive demand for a cup of tea following her.

Judy looked in on Sandra Myers but she still had her face to the wall and was apparently still crying. She did not respond when Judy asked if she wanted anything.

Judy reported to Marta that she honestly thought Sandra was psycho. Well, suffering post-natal depression. Or something. That gorgeous little baby – why didn't she want to see her? Marta said calmly that maybe her husband would have some answers. He'd just rung, having finally got Marta's message. He'd be there as soon as he could. Judy seemed sceptical. 'What if he's a psychopath?'

Marta thought it unlikely. Bernard Myers sounded like a nice man. He'd been worried sick about his wife and hadn't slept since she went missing. He was in Newcastle now, he'd gone there thinking she might be staying with a friend. Marta thought Terence should break the news to Sandra, since he was the one she seemed to trust most.

And with that Judy had to be content, especially as Miss Bird appeared at the door to Marta's office, positively begging for a cup of tea.

'All these nurses just lounging about,' she said.

'Surely one of them could make an old lady a cup of tea.'

'*All* these nurses? I'll have you know, Miss Bird, that we are currently under-staffed. We are two nurses short and we have no administrator. We are doing our best under very difficult circumstances!'

'Alright! I'll make it myself. It's not as though I'm totally helpless.' And she headed for the kitchen. Judy sighed and went after her.

It was mid-afternoon before Terence was able to see Sandra Myers. Her condition, or rather her state of mind, was not much improved. Marta hovered in the background.

'Matron tells me you've been crying a lot, Mrs Myers. And hardly eating at all. I'd prefer it were the other way around.' Sandra said nothing.

'I'm going to give you an injection of ergotamine, that'll help to shrink the uterus. As for the scar, it's healing nicely. It'll hardly show in a few months.' He got a faint nod. He told her he'd just checked on the baby and found Mrs. Lerici, who taught at the primary school, feeding her.

'She had a little girl too a few weeks ago, and she offered to help out,' Marta said.

'Tell her thank you,' was all Sandra said. Marta and Terence exchanged a look. Terence decided the time had come for some serious talk.

'Mrs Myers – Sandra – something is clearly upsetting you a great deal. We want to help if we can. Soon you'll have to make some very big decisions. I'd like to think they'll be the right ones.'

'They'll be my decisions, doctor. Right or wrong.'

'And they'll affect another human being, right or wrong. Maybe for a lifetime. That's a big responsibility.'

'My responsibility.'

'Perhaps so. But as a doctor, I have responsibilities too. For you and your baby. I've asked Matron to contact your husband. He's on his way. I hope you'll be willing to see him.'

Sandra looked at him with a mixture of fury and despair. 'I trusted you. I thought – here is one man who won't let me down. But no … you are all the same.' And she buried her head in the pillow and would not speak again.

Which left Terence, after the satisfaction of the successful surgery, feeling deflated and questioning whether, after all, they had been right to interfere. Marta was reassuring. For better or worse, Bernard Myers was coming. And no doubt they would work it out between them. He'd sounded thrilled about the baby so at the very least that little girl should end up with a home. Terence thought a home would be good but a family would be a damn sight better, and with that Marta could only agree.

Frank Gilroy, driving back to Wandin Valley after a meeting in Burrigan, was also thinking about family. He was thinking about Alma, his first wife, and his kids, Kevin and Lorraine, and how he missed having them all around. Not that you wanted grown-up children living at home, they had their own lives to lead. It's just that the house was so darn quiet … he was lonely, he admitted that. But it wasn't just loneliness driving his pursuit of Shirley Dean. So different to his dear old Alma – could it ever work out? That was the question that plagued him. His thoughts were rudely interrupted when a battered Holden Monaro roared past doing a speed that Frank considered an affront to civilised society. He recognised the car. But since Frank was stopped at the Burrigan turn-off T intersection, Peter Gleeson clearly had failed to see him. Frank turned on the siren and picked him up a few k's down the road. Young Peter was not pleased and felt that the sergeant was picking on him.

'Honestly, Sarge, I wasn't doing a click over eighty.'

'If that's what you reckon, Peter, either your eyesight's faulty or your speedo is.' He shook his head sadly. 'You kids. No judgement. No common sense either. You drive these overpowered cars, you put your foot down and the next minute you're flying. Nice sensation, I grant you – until you hit a power-pole.' Peter glowered. Frank continued his homily. 'Next time you won't be so lucky, son. Next time I'll have the radar, you'll be up for a big fine.'

'Won't be a next time.'

'Glad to hear it. 'Cause I figure your dad's got enough on his plate, he doesn't want to be burying his only son. So take it easy. You hear me?'

'Yes, Sarge.'

'I've got my eye on you, Peter. You and your mates, you're all the same. Pass the word.' He went back to the police car. He had the very strong sense that the sermon had fallen on deaf ears.

Feeling – rather like Terence – a lack of job satisfaction, Frank drove on towards Wandin Valley but his journey was again interrupted. An overladen station-wagon was parked by the side of the road and the young couple beside it appeared to be studying a map. Ever the good Samaritan, Frank stopped to help and learnt that here were the new owners of the Davidson place, Molly and Brendan Jones. He tried to ignore Molly's pink boiler suit and the several yellow ribbons in her hair – after all, his own Shirl loved bright colours (he was starting to think of her as 'his' Shirl which was probably not wise) – and he soon had them pointed in the right direction.

'Tell me,' Molly said to him, 'is it very run down?'

'What, the house?' said Frank.

'Well, everything.'

Frank didn't want to dampen their enthusiasm. 'Oh, you know. Needs a bit of work. Loads of character, though. I'm sure you'll soon settle in. Welcome to Wandin Valley!' And he waved them off, thinking, the Davidson place! God help them.

No one was helping Sandra Myers, though there were plenty of people willing to try. She had stopped crying and had sunk into a slough of despond, a black hole that was partly self-pity but more despair. She was acutely aware that everyone at the hospital thought she was difficult and probably selfish as well. Well it didn't matter what they thought. They didn't know what had happened to her, they had no idea how impossible her situation was. And not knowing, they had no right to judge. She lay there, tired and sore and lonely, trying to work out just how she would handle the next twenty-four hours. In fact, she had no idea.

Jenny Secombe, like Sandra, was faced with a dilemma at least partly of her own making and felt equally lost. She'd got the late bus home from Burrigan High, convincing herself that she needed to work in the library for an hour, and her father had started the milking by the time she got in, so chances for mature discussion – which was what she had in mind – were further delayed. She turned the radio on and started to prepare dinner. In between ads for sheep dip and tractors, Leo Sayer pumped out *More Than I Can Say* and Jenny hummed along and wondered why indeed her life should be filled with sorrow. As she put a tuna casserole in the oven, Kim Carnes took over with *Bette Davis Eyes* but failed to lift her mood to any significant degree. She heard Hal scraping his boots then removing them at the back door and tensed all over and hurried to turn the radio off as he came in, changing into the old loafers he kept by the back door.

'Good song, that. You don't have to turn it off.' Jenny just shrugged and left it off. 'You were late home.'

'I went to the library. Did some work.'

Hal thought she was probably avoiding him but he let it go. 'Something's up with the milking machine. Have to get Bob Hatfield out to look at it.'

'Does he know about milking machines?'

'Fixed it last time.'

'Fair enough. Dad, dinner'll be a while yet. Can we talk?'

Hal had been dreading this moment as much or more than Jenny herself. 'Okay.'

'I mean, we didn't get far last night. And you said you wanted to sleep on it. And I gave you all day as well …'

Hal wanted to say that he was hoping she might have come to her senses but since she obviously hadn't he said nothing.

'Well I guess you haven't changed your mind. And nor have I. I want see Dr Bowen and I want to go on the pill. I don't know what all the fuss is about. Tony and I want to make love and I don't want to get pregnant. I think I'm being responsible.'

'You're fifteen!' Hal sounded almost anguished.

'That's why I don't want to get pregnant, Dad.'

'How can you be sure you love him?'

'I just know. Like you knew you loved Mum.'

'We were adults.'

'Lots of adults make mistakes.'

Hal made a last, desperate plea. 'Couldn't you at least wait until you're sixteen?'

'What's the point? It's only a few months, what difference does it make?'

'It would please me. I love you, Jenny and I don't

want to see you get hurt.'

'If I can't get pregnant, how can I get hurt?'

He wanted to tell her: in a thousand ways, this is a teenage boy we're talking about, he's nowhere near as mature as you, he's totally self-centred, he's led by his dick, Jenny! But he couldn't bring himself to say it. What he said was, 'I'll give you a letter for Dr Bowen. But I want you to know I hate the very idea of it.'

This was not the way it was supposed to go. She wanted his blessing. *'Why?'*

'Because there's a time and a place for everything and this isn't the time and the back of that panel van isn't the place. I thought you'd get married in church one day. In a white dress, as beautiful as your mother was. But you'll be used goods, Jen – and who's going to want you?' He got up, stiffly, suddenly feeling old though he wasn't yet forty. 'I think I'll take another look at the milking machine. Wouldn't want it to break down in the morning.'

He went out. Jenny ran to her room and threw herself on her bed and sobbed as if her heart were breaking. In the oven, the tuna casserole slowly curled and blackened.

Had Shirley been cooking, a burnt tuna casserole might well have been on the menu at the Dean household but fortunately Vicky got home in time to try out a new chicken curry. She was busy putting it together – or rather, trying to make sense of the recipe – while Shirley took a phone call.

'Oh, Frank, if it's about the rust, any time – oh. Oh, I see. Well, that's very kind … Tomorrow? Yes, I'm free, I'd love to! … Yes, see you then. Thank you, Frank, bye now.' She looked at Vicky, rolled her eyes and escaped to her pyramid.

'Not so fast,' Vicky said. 'What now?'

'He's taking me to the club. Tomorrow night.'

Vicky was more than a little stunned. 'As in – you're going on a date?'

'Oh really, Vicky, must you make us sound like a couple of teenagers? He says there's a good band playing, that's all.'

'So I believe. But I thought you didn't want to encourage him.' Shirley admitted that was indeed the case. But since Frank seemed incapable of taking a hint, she'd decided she would have to tell him to his face. Vicky wondered about the wisdom of doing that in public. What if he got upset? Shirley said Frank was incapable of showing emotion. She'd tell him nicely she wasn't the girl for him and that would be that. Vicky thought perhaps she ought to do it in song. Make a big number out of it. Perhaps they should ask the band?

'What's this "we" business? You won't be there.'

'I will as it happens. I'm going with Hal Secombe.'

'Really?' That was enough to get Shirley out from under the pyramid again. While they waited for the chicken curry to cook, they discussed the pitfalls of raising kids on your own. They both thought Hal Secombe was doing a pretty good job, even if Jenny did not, at the present time, agree.

'I guess she's missing her mum,' Shirley said.

'Funny,' Vicky said. 'But I don't think I ever really missed Dad all that much.'

'He wasn't the sort to be missed,' Shirley said tartly, 'He never made himself sufficiently loveable when he was there.'

Vicky shook her head. 'How on earth did you ever get together in the first place?'

Free spirit though she was, Shirley didn't want to say it was a one night stand. Besides, it wasn't quite. Jack Dean was a friend of sorts, the local vet, she'd known him for years.

'Well?'

'I was twenty-three, only back from Europe a few months. And there was good old Jack. I would have gone off again, I wanted to find an Italian count, except I got pregnant to him instead.'

Vicky seemed surprised. 'You never told me that before.'

'I thought you'd have figured it out, you're supposed to be good at maths.'

'Never crossed my mind. Would you have married him if I hadn't happened along?'

'Probably not, to be perfectly honest. But I never, not once for a single moment, regretted having you.'

'I'm glad about that. Because you're definitely the best mum I ever had.' She grinned. 'And now you've got the local cop chasing you.'

'I know!' Shirley said, topping up their wine from the cask which Frank had saved from disaster. 'Where will it all end?'

CHAPTER TEN

For Molly and Brendan Jones, it was all just beginning: a new life in a new place a long way from the City of Churches. And they were wondering if perhaps they hadn't made a terrible mistake. They hadn't yet unpacked the station wagon. They hadn't dared. Their tour of inspection had left them momentarily wanting to climb back into it. The trouble was that the farm had become too much for old Fred Davidson years before he finally gave in and moved to live with his daughter on the central coast of New South Wales. Now it looked rundown, worn-out and totally unloved. Fences sagged, paint peeled, windows gaped open and weeds ran riot. The outdoor dunny was clearly attempting to rival the Leaning Tower of Pisa.

'Character. That's what that cop said. I think I could find a different word.' Molly sounded close to tears and Brendan felt he should make an effort before they both fell apart.

'The house isn't that bad. At least it's clean.' And it was. The agent must have attended to that. Barely liveable, but clean. 'And whatshername, Doris, she seemed friendly enough.'

'She barely blinked when I said hello.'

'Moll? We're tired. Let's get the stuff inside and put the kettle on. We're here in one piece, it's going to be good, I know it is.'

'I'm sorry. I'm being silly. It's not that bad really. I mean – we knew it was rundown and everything … we'll fix it up.'

'Of course we will.'

'And at least the lino isn't so bad.'

'Almost tasteful.'

Just as well the two of them had vast stores of optimism, they would find it useful in the days ahead. A couple of hours later, the car was unpacked and the house was full of boxes. A van would arrive with the rest of their stuff the next day.

'Where on earth is it all going to go?' Molly wondered.

Brendan had been opening Caroline's farewell present. 'More to the point – where on earth is *this* going to go?'

From dozens of layers of packaging, he finally extracted a large chandelier. Molly stared in amazement. Brendan handed her the card that came with it and she read aloud: 'To Melissa and Brendan – Just remember, even in the boondocks, style's the thing! Love, Caroline.'

'I worry about your mother,' said Brendan.

'I've got just the spot for it,' said Molly. 'Didn't you notice how dull Doris's sty is?'

Restored to their usual cheerfulness by the silliness of it all, they resumed unpacking. It's doubtful whether Caroline would have been gratified to know that her gift had had such a salutary effect.

***

Terence had called at the hospital to see a patient. He thought of visiting Sandra Myers again but decided it was pointless trying to pressure her further. Instead, he checked on her progress with Marta Kurtesz.

'She's just the same, Terence. Barely touched her dinner. Heaven knows what sort of a reception her husband is going to get.'

'Do we know when he's likely to get here?'

'He didn't want to arrive in the middle of the night. He said he'd come first thing tomorrow.' She sighed. She sounded tired, Terence thought; her accent always became just a little more pronounced when she was tired.

'Can't you go home?' he asked.

'There's a meeting of the Ladies Auxiliary. I promised Elaine I'd pop in. Explain to them how badly we need a new ECG machine.'

'You work too hard.'

'I haven't had much choice, we've been under-staffed. Fortunately, the situation should ease a little tomorrow.'

'Tomorrow?'

'I've got a new nurse starting.'

'Experienced?'

'Very. Trained in the city. Double certificated.'

'Excellent. Married?' He added quickly, 'First thing Simon will ask.'

'As a matter of fact, yes.' She was smiling.

'What aren't you telling me?' But a baby started to cry and Marta was quickly on her feet.

'Marta! Let someone else go.'

'Judy's left. And Ruth Hammond doesn't have much of a knack with babies. I do wonder though, how Mrs Myers can lie there, listening ...' She shrugged. 'Goodnight, Terence.' And she was gone. Terence went home, wondering about Bernie Myers making the long drive south, hoping to God he didn't fall asleep at the wheel; wondering why, when you had a good thing going as no doubt those two did, it could so easily become a train-wreck. And he thought, wryly, that he of all people should have the answers.

The valley was still bathed in moonlight when Andy Mackay took the first tray of high tin white from the oven. Andy was an old-fashioned country baker and a very good one; his bread was famous for miles around, people detoured off the highway to buy his pies, he'd done well enough to have two boys in boarding school. He was, as they say, happy with his lot; he didn't even mind getting up at three o'clock six days a week. He checked the temperature, slid the multigrain on to the rack and closed the oven door again just as Elaine came in carrying two cups of coffee. He was both surprised and delighted to see her.

'What are you doing up?'

'Couldn't sleep for some reason. It was a pretty heated meeting last night. And I didn't get what I wanted.'

Andy smiled. 'But you will.'

'We'll see.' She passed him the coffee. 'Where's Steve?' Steve was the apprentice and not usually late.

'On his way. Had a flat.'

Elaine nodded. 'Happens. Can I help?'

'No, no. I'm right. Coffee's brilliant though.' He went on shaping croissants, thinking how good it was to see her here, in the bakery. It was separate to the house, an old brick building with the shop in front. Because of the hours he kept, they didn't actually spend all that much time together, Andy thought, but it didn't matter, it was still a good marriage, the best.

'I bumped into Ian yesterday,' he said now, 'at the service station.'

'Ian? Ian Sutton?' She sounded a bit startled, but

Andy thought she was probably not quite awake yet. He grinned.

'How many Ians do we know? I thought it was time we had him round for a meal.'

'Oh. Yes. If you like. Have to be Sunday lunch, though.'

'Or Saturday night.' The bakery was closed on Sundays.

'Not next Saturday. Lions Club dinner. I'll see what we can organise. I'd better go and have a shower. Don't work too hard.' She gave Andy a quick kiss on the cheek, stopped for a moment to pat the Jack Russell and was gone.

Later, but not much later, Molly Jones was out searching for something which might constitute breakfast for a large sow. She was about to settle for several armloads of dandelions but fortunately for Doris found a sugarbag in the barn with 'PIG FOOD' scrawled across it. It contained pellets of some sort. Molly had been reading up, she intended to farm organically and was not big on pellets but didn't believe in starving animals either. She tipped some into Doris's trough. Doris did not even react. So much for pigs being greedy. Or perhaps she was just a late riser. She certainly seemed unmoved by the chandelier now gracing her sty.

Molly went back inside and found Brendan showered and dressed and about to put breakfast on the table. She wondered if he was feeling nervous, first day in a new job, and he admitted to feeling a slight twinge of apprehension. It was going to be very different to what he was used to but he was rather looking forward to the change of pace.

He was worried about leaving her alone but Molly declared that *she* wasn't nervous in the least. And she did, after all, have a large pig to protect her. They both, it seemed, felt a great deal more cheerful about the prospect before them.

Vicky Dean already knew a little about the new people at the Davidson place. 'I forgot to tell you last night, Mum,' she was saying, interrupting Shirley's early morning meditations. 'Your Sergeant Gilroy found them when he was coming back from Burrigan. They'd got themselves lost.'

'He is not *my* Sergeant Gilroy.'

'A young couple from the city, apparently. I thought I'd pop out and introduce myself.'

'Just being neighbourly?'

'Mm. That too.' Shirley gave her a look. 'They inherited that pig of old Fred's, Mum. Maybe I can drum up a bit of business. You haven't eaten that chocolate cake Mrs. Marks gave me yesterday, have you?'

'Would I steal your cake?'

'You usually do. I thought I'd take it to them. Let them know the natives are friendly.' Shirley wondered aloud if the property was really a financial proposition and Vicky shook her head. She'd had the same thought. She hoped the Joneses had another source of income because she wouldn't want to be living off that farm herself. Not for the next few years anyway. You'd have to be mad to try. But then if it didn't rain soon the whole district would be in trouble.

At Wandin Valley Hospital, Marta Kurtesz was clock-watching, wondering how soon Bernie Myers might arrive. She did not really expect him yet; he'd sounded a little apprehensive when she'd last spoken to him. Marta sensed that the forthcoming meeting with his wife would not be an easy one. She steeled herself and went to see Sandra, putting on a bright face.

'Good morning, Sandra,' she said as she walked in, 'I

know we need rain but it really is the most beautiful morning! Aren't you going to eat your breakfast?'

'I had some toast.'

'A new mother needs a bit more than toast.' She started to do Sandra's obs while she chatted. 'You know, I went for a ride this morning, I've got this big bay gelding called The General. And I couldn't help thinking how lucky we are in this country. A great climate, wide open spaces ... so much freedom. I heard from my uncle in Hungary this week and he said it's been a shocking winter, really bitter. It made me glad that I'm here.'

'Do you ever get homesick?'

'Well of course. Sometimes. Nothing's ever perfect, is it? We have to look for the good side, wherever we are. And I have much to be thankful for.' She paused for just a moment. 'As do you, Sandra.'

It was a while before Sandra spoke. 'Why did you ring him?'

'You're an intelligent woman. You know the answer to that. You have a child who needs to be cared for.'

'When will he be here?'

'Quite soon, I should think.'

'I don't intend to see him.'

Marta sighed. 'Well I don't suppose we can make you.'

'If he wants the baby, he can have her.'

Marta gave up then. 'I'll get Sister Loveday to come and help you wash.' And she went out without another word.

Left alone again, Sandra sat up and tried to swing her legs out of the bed but groaned with the pain. She sat on the edge of the bed, trying to catch her breath, then she started to fumble with the IV line attached to her arm.

Marta had found Judy in the nursery, feeding the baby with milk expressed by Mrs. Lerici.

'Do you think she means it?' Judy asked. 'She really

wants him to take the baby?'

'I think Sandra Myers is hurting badly. And there has to be a way to break through that, if only we knew how.'

'She's not making it easy,' Judy said, with considerable understatement. 'Want me to have a go?'

'Feel free,' Marta said, 'it can't do any harm. Oh, by the way, we've got a new nurse starting later this morning. That should make things a little easier.'

'Experienced?' Judy asked, tucking Baby Myers up in the humidicrib.

'Very.'

'Thank God for that.'

In her room, Sandra was still having trouble with the IV line. She heard Judy calling out to Miss Bird, something about a cup of tea, and panicked. She ripped the line out of her arm, wincing with the pain, ignoring the thin trickle of blood, and stopping only to grab her handbag, fled out of the room.

CHAPTER ELEVEN

Elaine Mackay, who had accomplished so much during her years in Wandin Valley, was not the sort of woman to leave unfinished business in her wake. Which is why she had called at the hospital to see her friend, Marta Kurtesz, to apologise for the fiasco at last night's meeting of the Ladies' Auxiliary. Marta had been very eloquent and Elaine had been quite sure that funds would be found for a new ECG machine but others had different ideas and she'd been unable to win the day. Still, she was optimistic that it would all happen before too long; she wanted to leave Marta with some hope. It was as she got out of her car that she saw Sandra Myers, dressed in nothing but a hospital gown and clutching her Prada handbag, make her way as fast as she could to the yellow Mercedes. Elaine thought for just a moment that she was hallucinating. Then, as Sandra got into the car and put the key in the ignition, she sprang into action and raced to stop her.

'My dear Sandra, this time I'm absolutely sure you shouldn't be driving. Please, do be a sensible girl and give me the keys.' And being Elaine, she simply leant in and took the keys while Sandra slumped over the wheel. 'Come on now,' Elaine said gently, 'whatever it is, it is almost certainly not as bad as you think. But your arm's bleeding a little, do you think we could go back inside?'

By the time Marta and Judy came running, Elaine had Sandra out of the car and was helping her, sobbing, back towards the hospital. Not a lot was said as the little procession moved slowly inside. Miss Bird, however, was not impressed. Waiting in the corridor, she vented her feelings.

'There is always some drama in this hospital!' she said. 'Anything to prevent a poor old woman getting a cup of tea!'

Miss Bird was ignored. Judy took Sandra to her room. Marta had a word to Elaine, who apologised profusely about the ECG machine but said she still had a few ideas she'd discuss with Shirley Dean. Marta smiled. 'I don't know where you get your energy.'

'I like to keep busy, Marta. I've enjoyed my work with the Auxiliary, it's been quite a challenge. And we have had a few successes.'

'That sounds a bit final. You're not going to resign in a fit of pique?'

'Not a chance. Well, I hope you can help Sandra sort things out.'

'Yes,' said Marta, 'for a woman to leave her child – she must have been very badly hurt.'

And then Elaine said something which did not make sense to Marta until a great deal later. 'People are sometimes driven to choices which others find incomprehensible. We have to accept that. See you later, my dear.' She kissed Marta and left, and Marta went once more to see if she could, indeed, help Sandra to 'sort things out'.

Judy had dressed Sandra's arm and put a new cannula

in. Marta went in and sat beside the bed. She took Sandra's hand in hers.

'You nearly gave me a heart attack.'

'I wish you'd let me go.'

'You know we can't do that. We don't want you dying on us.'

Finally Sandra turned to her. 'You don't understand. I don't care. He doesn't love me any more. He's got someone else.'

Such an old, old story, Marta thought. And pretty much what she'd expected. She sighed and patted Sandra's hand in sympathy and asked her to please just stay in bed. No one would force her see her husband. Then she went to bring Terence up to date. He felt guilty again about the call to the husband, though they really hadn't had much choice, and promised to drop in at the hospital later in the morning. Marta was barely off the phone when Nurse Hammond arrived with Brendan Jones. Marta's welcome was little short of effusive.

'Mr Jones, I am delighted to see you. It's good of you to start so quickly but as I think you understand, we are close to desperate.'

'Not a problem, Matron, I'm glad to be here.'

'You've settled in to the Davidson place alright?'

'Well – early days. We only arrived late yesterday.'

'And soon of course the whole town will be calling it the Jones' place.'

Brendan laughed but before they got much further, Simon arrived.

'Ah, Doctor Bowen,' Marta said. 'This is Mr Jones, he and his wife have moved onto the Davidson place.'

'Oh, great. Nice to meet you.' They shook hands.

'Can I help you with something, doctor?' Marta smiled, knowing full well why Simon was there. 'Mrs. Blackman seems just fine this morning.'

'Oh, well I thought I should pop in and check. And

Terence mentioned you've got a new nurse starting? City girl?'

Marta laughed. 'City *boy*, Dr Bowen.' Simon realised that Brendan was grinning and the penny dropped.

'Good Lord, you'll have the tongues wagging for months! Welcome on board, mate. Though I was hoping for someone with better legs. Where did you train?'

'The Queen Vic in Adelaide.'

'Really? Ever run into Robert Bowen?'

'*The* Robert Bowen? Who entered the operating theatre to a fanfare of trumpets?'

'Sounds altogether possible. My old man.' Brendan was suitably and sincerely astonished and they were just settling in for the sort of gossip session that medical people are only too fond of when Miss Bird appeared with her usual exquisite timing. Simon found he was urgently needed elsewhere.

'Ever been droving?' he muttered enigmatically to Brendan and disappeared.

'Looks like you're in for a baptism of fire,' Marta murmured to Brendan. She turned to Miss Bird and smiled brightly. 'Miss Bird, I want to introduce you to someone. Meet Mr Jones. Your new nurse.'

Miss Bird was flabbergasted. 'He's not a nurse.'

'Oh yes he is,' said Marta.

'Oh yes I am,' said Brendan simultaneously.

'I've heard of this sort of thing,' said Miss Bird. 'In the city. But I never thought I'd live to see it in Wandin Valley. It's not decent.'

'Miss Bird, I'm a very good nurse. I'll look after you very well. Now let's get you back to bed, shall we?' And he scooped her up in his arms quite effortlessly and carried her, protesting, in Marta's wake. The funny thing was that after a moment or two he felt tiny Miss Bird relax in his arms and he thought, it might be forty years since a man held her but once upon a time she enjoyed it. And he told her as much and she actually smiled. Marta, overhearing, thought Brendan Jones might be quite an asset to the team and in that her judgement would be proved correct.

Back at the surgery, Simon did not feel that he was living up to the illustrious Bowen name. That is, the conundrum presented by Tim Bourke's migraines was still unsolved. Tim had obligingly returned, at Simon's request, for a second consultation, before dashing off to hopefully take a few wickets in the scheduled match against Eugowra High. Simon was checking the family history once again and had failed to unearth, amongst Tim large horde of relatives, a single case of asthma or allergy, of wheezes or rashes or hives or spots – though Tim himself had contracted measles at the age of four or thereabouts. He was spotty then, he said helpfully.

'So you've been getting migraines for four years, every Monday morning.'

'Pretty much.'

'Any Mondays when you didn't get it?'

Tim thought possibly one or two but he seemed doubtful. Simon asked about school holidays but Tim said he still got it even then. Simon looked surprised.

'I'd have thought that busted the idea about it being connected to school, then.'

Tim nodded. 'Exactly what I always said.' He thought for a moment. 'It was funny last year though, when Dad went to America ... I didn't have a migraine all the time he was away.'

Simon tried to suppress his excitement. For a moment he saw, not Tim but poor Jenny Secombe sitting opposite him. He thought at last, we're on to something, classic parent-teenager conflict. He tried to keep his voice casual. 'And when your dad came home?'

'Yeah, the headaches came back.'

'The two of you – how do you get on?'

'Me and Dad? Great. He's terrific, he drives me to all the my games – takes half the team, sometimes.'

'What happens when you lose?' Simon had visions of the ugly parent, ruthlessly forcing his kid on, but Tim just grinned.

'Dad just says to get over it, you can't expect to win them all.'

'So you never argue?'

'Not much. Only when I play music too loud.'

Simon deflated. It did not appear that Tim's dad was the problem. 'Which I'm betting doesn't happen on Mondays.'

Tim was suddenly serious. 'Nope. Not on Mondays. This migraine thing – I feel like such a wuss, you know? And I get a lot of sh – I get teased a lot. I reckon if I wasn't quite good at sport I'd really get bullied. But I don't think it's – what do you call it? Psychological? I mean, you're the doctor. But I just think there's some other cause.'

Simon, who thought Tim was one bright kid, was inclined to agree with him. And more determined than ever to find out what that cause was.

In the car park at the hospital, a black Mercedes eased in beside the yellow one. 'Well I never,' said Miss Bird, peering through her window, 'are we being honoured by a visit from royalty?' Brendan, who was now in uniform and had been giving her a backrub, confirmed that it was not Prince Charles who alighted.

It was in fact a weary and rather rumpled-looking Bernard Myers. He was met at the hospital entrance by a less than friendly Judy Loveday and taken to Marta's office.

'Mr Myers, Matron. Here at last.' Marta gave her a look that would freeze hell over.

'Thank you, Sister, I think that's Miss Bird wanting attention, is it not?' Judy vanished at speed. Marta held out her hand to Bernard.

'Mr Myers, I'm Marta Kurtesz, we spoke on the phone. What a trip you've had. Please do sit down.'

'Thank you. I'm sorry I look so dishevelled, I haven't slept since I found she'd gone. Phone calls to everyone I could think of, hospitals, police, I even rang the morgue. And then I went to see her friend in Newcastle, I was out of my mind, I –'

'Please – there's no need to apologise.'

'How is she? And the baby, a little girl, you said. Can I see them?'

'My Myers, you can see your little girl in just a moment. But your wife – that's a different matter. Sandra won't see you or the baby. She says she wants nothing to do with either of you.'

He sat there in stunned silence. He had not expected this and it took some time to digest. He looked completely shattered, Marta thought. She couldn't help feeling some sympathy for him.

'Me, I can understand,' he said finally. 'I've treated her so badly. But the baby?'

'I think, in her mind, the two of you are inextricably linked. You wanted a girl, isn't that right?' He nodded. 'You got what you wanted, she sees it – and I don't think she's being quite rational, we're not always, when we are hurt – as just another example of you getting your own way.'

'If I could just have a minute with her. A chance to explain.'

'Not until she says so. She's feeling very unloved.'

'*Unloved?*'

'She says you have found someone else.'

'But it's not like that at all!'

Marta wondered what it *was* like but he just sighed

and shook his head and asked if he could please see his daughter and she took him to the nursery. Like all new fathers, he looked at the little red bundle in wonder and awe. He asked about the humidicrib, was she okay, and Marta explained about the prematurity and her tiny lungs, she'd be out of there and on her own tomorrow most likely, she was doing really well.

'She's beautiful, just like her mother.' He turned to Marta. 'I'll get a room at the motel. I'll stay until Sandra agrees to see me. I have to see her. I want to apologise. I want her to know that I love her. That there's no one else, no one at all. I did one stupid thing, Matron, and I'll do anything I can to make up for it. Can you tell her that?'

'I'll do my best,' Marta said.

She hoped for the baby's sake that she had the necessary skills for her new role of marriage guidance counsellor. Or maybe she'd hand the job to Terence. Bernard seemed to sense her reluctance. 'Perhaps I should tell you the whole sordid story.'

'There's no need,' Marta said, too quickly.

'Sandy and me, we're in the rag trade. She designs, I sell. We're good. So a couple of nights ago I was at the Fashion Awards Dinner. It was televised, I don't suppose you watched it?' Marta shook her head. 'Normally Sandra would have been there but this year she didn't feel up to it. Anyway, we won the resort wear – huge thrill – and Sandra saw it all. She also saw me with Lynette.'

Marta didn't really need to hear any more but he went on anyway, no doubt finding it cathartic. 'I lived with Lynette for a while, before I met Sandra. Well of course we partied afterwards and I got drunk and I ended up back at Lynette's and sometime early next morning the phone rang and I foolishly answered it …'

'And when you got home she was gone?'

Bernard nodded. 'I love Sandra, Matron. I know I've stuffed up – oh, God, have I ever, but I love her. And I want to try again. You know the stupidest part of all this? I can't even remember if I actually had sex with Lynette or not?'

'But the intention was there.' Marta wasn't in the mood for excuses.

'Oh I'm sure it probably was. At the time. But it all seems so crass, doesn't it? Imagine if I lost the woman I love – and that little girl – over something like that?' His anguish was real and Marta softened. But she didn't remind him that at the moment he appeared in no danger of losing his daughter.

Simon Bowen was sitting on the edge of Terence's desk, seeking a second opinion – second to his own, that is. The problem of Tim Bourke's migraines, though hardly life-threatening, was nagging away at him.

'The thing is,' Simon was saying, 'Tim says he actually likes school.'

'So where's the stress?'

'Exactly. And he does seem pretty well-adjusted. Keeping up with the work, girlfriend, lots of sport.'

'And there's no family history?'

'Not a damn thing. No asthma, no allergies, nothing.'

'Still – one does keep thinking histamines?'

'Well I was, yes. I'm glad you are too.'

Terence grinned. 'You're treating this as a real challenge, aren't you?'

'Got to prove that six years of study achieved something. Other than a pretty piece of paper, that is. Thanks, Terence.'

'No problem. Oh, do you think you could make a couple of house calls for me this afternoon? I could be a bit tied up with the Sandra Myers case.'

'Love to.'

'Well I don't know if you'll love it, exactly. Oh, Jill Benson's okay, you've seen her before, but there's Vernon Locke as well, known to all as Cookie – have you met him yet?' Simon shook his head. 'Runs the club and doesn't do a bad job either. Wait till you try his Gemfish Cleopatra –'

'His *what*?'

'Treat in store. Anyway, he's got a badly infected leg which he won't stay off and I'm really quite concerned about him. If you'd just check him out, make sure he's taking the damn penicillin? There'd be rioting in the streets if anything happened to Cookie. Well from some quarters; Esme Watson would probably offer up a quiet prayer of thanks.'

Simon was beginning to realise what a lot he had still to learn about the good folk of Wandin Valley. He greeted Elaine Mackay on his way through reception. She was having a cup of tea with Shirley – and, of course, admiring the latest floral offering.

'He does know how to grow roses, Shirley, you've got to give him that.' Shirley sniffed. 'Oh come on, he's a nice man!'

'*My* sort of man?'

'Well. Maybe not. But then – is this really your sort of town?'

Shirley was surprised by that. 'It's home, darling. I was born and raised here.'

'So why are you always rushing off somewhere else?'

'Am I? Well I suppose I am. Up to a point.'

'I think,' said Elaine, 'you find it quite stifling at times. Like I do.'

Shirley knew that it was true. 'Look. I've just sent off for some brochures, a ten-day bicycle tour of southern China. Why don't we go together?'

'Are you serious?'

'Of course! Doesn't it sound interesting? Andy could

manage without you.'

'I'll give it some thought. Since I can't imagine anyone better to cycle around China with. And now I really have to be off. Goodbye, my crazy friend. I love you, Shirley Dean.' They shared a warm hug. Then Shirley waved at the teacups.

'You don't want a reading before you go?'

Elaine laughed. 'Not just now. I know exactly what's in store for me today!' But in that she could not have been more wrong.

CHAPTER TWELVE

Judy was attending to the baby in the nursery. Marta, having finally had a chance to give Brendan a quick tour of inspection, stopped with him there.

'You did meet Sister Loveday?'

Judy grinned. 'We had half a cup of coffee somewhere.'

Marta smiled. 'One of those days and it's not even lunchtime. Though that one thinks it is.'

Brendan cooed at the baby. 'She's doing well for – what did you say? Four weeks prem?' Judy nodded. 'And the mother hasn't even seen her?'

'Completely refuses. But maybe things will change in the next twenty-four hours.'

Marta and Brendan moved on to Marta's office. 'So? What do you think?'

Brendan smiled. 'I'm impressed. For a small country hospital, you're remarkably well equipped.'

'We can thank Elaine Mackay for most of that. Oh, she has her band of helpers – but she's the driving force. Now she's trying to get us a new ECG machine. Before the current one electrocutes somebody.'

'Let's hope she succeeds.'

'Oh, she will. She'll have raffles and cake-stalls if she has to. But people here are generous. And very proud of their hospital.'

'It sounds like we've chosen a good town.'

'I think you have. There's a great sense of community, Brendan. And from what I've seen, you'll fit in fine.'

Unlike Brendan, Molly was feeling very much on her own, out on the Tallebung Road. They had agreed, she and Brendan, that the farm would be her domain and as she inspected it that first morning she tried to stay cheerful. Phrases from the agent's brochure – like 'picturesque rural retreat' – came back to mock her. There was too much rusty iron, too many sagging fences, too many acres of weeds for anyone to call it 'picturesque'. And yet, the ugly old sheds were softened by some quite magnificent peppercorn trees and the orchard, now overgrown and probably full of snakes, would no doubt respond to a pruning saw, while the line of willows that marked the creek were truly beautiful. Molly loved willows. But then, as if to offset the largesse of nature, down the back of the garden by the dilapidated chook yard stood the dunny. Ah, the fabled outdoor dunny, subject of so much Australian bush lore and literature and destined, in this case, to become the bane of Molly's life. An unlovely thing built of corrugated iron, from which the paint had long ago faded, it leant on a precarious angle toward the west. Little light penetrated and the bougainvillea clinging to its roof had not sufficient scent to dispel its overpowering odour. Inside, there were just enough cobwebs to remind the occupant of a certain well-loved song about redback spiders. Had Molly known about the dunny before she and Brendan bought the farm, it would very likely have been a deal-breaker. But she didn't know and here she was forced to use it. Tomorrow she would make sure she went before Brendan left. That way, if she fell into the bottomless pit, at least someone might hear her cries.

But the problem of the dunny was soon forgotten; Molly had a far bigger and far more pressing calamity to deal with, something which life in the city had ill-prepared her to deal with. It was, in fact, a catastrophe and caused her to give way to tears. Even a cup of camomile tea did nothing to staunch the flow; she was still crying when Vicky Dean arrived at the door half an hour later and introduced herself, trying to ignore – as Frank had done – Molly's striped leotard, Flamingo Park Sloppy Joe and glittered gum boots.

'A vet?' said Molly. 'Well it's nice to meet you, but you're too late.'

'Sorry?'

Molly wiped her eyes and tried to stop crying. 'I feel such a failure. Our second day here and already I've lost the only livestock we had.'

'Not Doris?' Molly nodded. 'Do you want to show me?'

'If you like,' said Molly. 'But I don't know what you can do for a dead pig.' As they walked out to Doris's sty, Molly explained what had happened; how Doris hadn't budged when she'd given the pig her breakfast and then later she'd found her just lying there, motionless.

'I gave her pellets, I hadn't had time to get anything else. Do you think they killed her?'

'I doubt it,' said Vicky, quite calmly.

'Rotten thing, why did she have to die on me? Just because she didn't like me! How on earth am I going to bury her? I mean – look at the size of her!'

They had reached the pen and were looking. 'I don't

think you'll have to bury her,' said Vicky.

'What? I can't leave her there to rot, can I? Poor thing.'

Vicky sighed. 'This is typical.' She yelled: 'Doris! Get off your fat behind and say hello! It's Vicky!'

The pig grunted and raised her head and finally, slowly, staggered to her feet. Molly turned to Vicky in amazement. 'Are you a miracle worker or something?' Vicky just laughed.

'Doris sulks. You'll get used to her little ways. Oh, by the way – she won't be needing a night light, pigs like to sleep.' It took Molly a moment to realise Vicky was referring to the chandelier, now installed in Doris's pen.

'Oh,' she said. 'My mother gave it to us. Tea? Coffee?'

'Love some. I've got a chocolate cake to go with it.'

'I think you're going to be my favourite vet,' said Molly, then turned for a parting shot at Doris. 'Don't imagine I'll forget this, Doris. I don't like pigs who sulk. It's very – unporcine.'

Vicky hid a smile. She thought Molly Jones was utterly crazy but likeable. Back in the kitchen, while Molly made tea on the portable gas stove, they chatted.

'I'm sorry about the mess but as you probably know, we only got here yesterday.'

'You haven't got the wood stove going yet?'

'I haven't dared try. It looks like it might be temperamental.'

'Oh, you'll soon get used to it. And the generator.' Vicky was eyeing the books in an open tea-chest. 'Who belongs to the medical tomes?'

'Brendan. He's a nurse, he's working at the hospital.'

'Already? Gosh, you don't waste any time, do you?' Vicky grinned and held up another volume. 'And this one? *History and Class Consciousness*?'

'Me. I was doing political science until this job came

up at Twiggies – big fashion house in Adelaide ...' She shrugged.

'Bye bye, pol sci.'

'I'm afraid so.'

Vicky looked at Molly's gear again. 'I can't say I'm surprised. Are you quite sure you're ready for life in the sticks?'

'Oh yes! I just hope the sticks are ready for me!'

If Vicky had doubts, she kept them to herself. 'So what are your plans, exactly? For the farm, I mean?'

Molly launched in. She didn't want people thinking that she and Brendan were just a couple of city drop-outs. They were absolutely determined to make a go of it. She unrolled a chart, showing Vicky their goals for the next twelve months; she waved at the books already unpacked, all of which she'd read – everything from *Life On A Small Planet* to *Raising Pigs for Fun and Profit*.

'That's great,' said Vicky, 'but what about practical experience?'

Molly remained upbeat. 'None at all. But I'm young and healthy, I'm energetic and unbearably optimistic. I reckon that'll do it.'

Vicky didn't have the heart to disillusion her. Instead, she forced an encouraging smile. 'Then I guess it's up to us locals to help where we can. You do know the land's pretty worn out?'

Molly looked astonished. 'Is it?'

'You haven't had any soil tests done yet?'

'Should I?'

'I think,' said Vicky, 'That we might be here for quite a while.'

Marta, whose goal for the day was family reunification, had spent some more time with Sandra Myers. It had not gone well. They had chatted about the baby, or rather Marta had chatted and Sandra had ignored her. Then

Sandra had asked, straight out, if her husband had arrived. When told he'd gone to book into the motel, she'd become very angry indeed.

'Tell him he's wasting his time! I will not see him!'

'I wish you'd think again about that,' Marta said.

'If you knew what he'd done …!'

'I do know. He told me everything.'

'And swore it was the first time and it would never happen again?'

'No, he said he treated you very badly but he loved you and he wanted to try again. He seemed – to me – to be full of remorse.'

'Remorse is not what he is full of. And I do not want to try again. You can tell him please that what I want is a divorce.'

And that, Marta was now telling Terence, was as far as they got. Neither could see much point in Terence making another attempt. Instead, he went to give the baby a complete check up. If all was still going well, she'd be out of the humidicrib tomorrow. And that could be a very good thing all round. Marta, getting his drift, agreed.

Simon Bowen was still chuckling over his earlier visit to an irascible Vernon Locke as he drove back to town. In his pocket was a voucher for a complimentary dinner for two at the Wandin Valley RSL Club – an indication that Vernon, or Cookie as Simon was calling him by the time he left – had warmed to the new doctor. He wondered if Vicky was keen on – what was it called? Ah yes, 'Gemfish Cleopatra'. His smile faded when he saw something on the bend up ahead, where a sign proclaimed 'Five Mile Creek'. He slowed down and came to a stop near the crash site, grabbed his bag and was out of his car and running. A man and a woman in a station-wagon had ploughed into a tree. A kid in a

Monaro, skewed off the road. And Sergeant Frank
Gilroy, who looked at him like he was some sort of
miracle.

'Simon, thank God. How the hell did you get here?'

'On my way back to town. What've we got?'

'You tell me. I reckon the kid's not too bad, Gleeson.
It's those two.' He indicated the station wagon. 'Elaine
Mackay and Ian Sutton.'

Molly was by now giving Vicky a tour of the farm, with
a bit of her life story thrown in. 'I woke up in hospital
with a leg in plaster and three broken ribs and there was
this handsome nurse with more curls than I've got doing
my obs. He looked down at me and said, "Melissa's a bit
of a mouthful, I'll call you Molly" and that was it.'

'That was Brendan?'

'Mm. Love at first sight. I thought we'd put a new pen
for the chickens over there and let them roam free in the
day time. Free range eggs are so much better, don't you
think? Those lovely orange yolks?'

Vicky smiled. 'Those lovely orange yolks are caused
by carotenoids in the diet. You could keep your chooks
in a cage and feed them marigold petals and you'd get
lovely orange yolks.'

'Oh. I guess I've got a bit to learn.' She looked at
Vicky. 'Where do you think would be a good spot for
the veggie garden? Or should I wait till I get the soil
checked?'

'Spot on, you're learning already, Molly Jones.'

They heard a siren then, away in the distance but still
insistent, cutting into the day.

'Ambulance?' Molly asked.

'Yeah. The fire siren's quite different, three rising
notes. If you hear that you ring Bev and see where it is.'

'Bev?'

'Beverley Little. Runs the telephone exchange. She's

shameless, listens in to everybody.'

The siren grew fainter. Molly shivered. 'I hate that sound. It used to give me nightmares when Brendan worked in Emergency. It always means trouble for someone, doesn't it?'

'Nearly always.'

There was certainly trouble at Five Mile Creek. While they waited for the ambulance, Simon did what he could for the crash victims. Ian Sutton's car – which had the name of his business, 'Sutton's Stock Feed, Eugowra', on the side – was a write-off. Ian himself, as far as Simon could see, had a head injury and at least a broken leg. He was actually more concerned about Elaine Mackay. She was grey-faced with rapid, shallow breathing. While he couldn't see any external injuries, he didn't like the look of her at all, he knew she must be haemorrhaging internally.

'Where's that damn ambulance?' he said rhetorically. He turned to Frank. 'Can you radio the hospital direct, Frank?'

'Sure.'

'Better warn them to get the theatre ready, in that case.'

Frank nodded and headed for the police car.

'Hey,' Peter Gleeson called. Frank paused, took a few steps towards him. 'My chest hurts.'

'Broken ribs,' said Frank, who had seen the Monaro's skid marks and found it hard to waste too much sympathy on Peter. 'They'll mend.'

'And look what they done to me car.' His voice was just slightly slurred. Frank looked. The Monaro was not too badly damaged. What he saw were the last three cans from a six-pack rolling around on the floor. He shook his head in disgust, he'd deal with that later, and went to call the hospital.

CHAPTER THIRTEEN

Jenny Secombe and Tony Pieri also heard the ambulance as it was heading back in to the hospital. They were lying on a towel by the swimming hole, the big one which all the kids frequented. It was not far from town and had been improved by the addition of a makeshift diving board and a tyre on a rope attached to an overhanging she-oak. The grass around it had mostly died off from being overused as a car park, but that possibly lessened the chance of meeting a red-bellied black in the water.

It had not been a good day for Jenny. She had barely slept and had avoided conversation with her dad as much as possible. She could tell he was upset too; she knew he wanted to reach out to her but she wouldn't let him, she didn't want to start crying again, she'd spent most of the night doing that. So breakfast had been a monosyllabic affair and she had left the house as soon as possible. It was Saturday, there was no school to occupy her. Instead she went to her friend Louise's house with the aim of getting some peer advice but once there realised this was a matter she could not discuss with anyone, not even her best friend. So they just chatted and played some music for a while and then Jenny cycled off to meet Tony, as she'd promised, and here they were, lying on the towel. The other kids were larking about around them and the sun was beating down, hot on their bare skin, and the siren sounded like doom in the background.

She had told him about the letter her father would write for Dr Bowen over the weekend; she'd make an appointment to get the prescription on Monday. Tony had seemed pretty pleased about all that. He kissed her shoulder and slid his hand under the edge of her bikini top and fondled her breast. She was embarrassed.

'Tony! Not where everyone can see!'

He laughed. 'Who's looking?' But he took his hand away. He suggested going to the drive-in again that night. Jenny was reluctant.

'It's *The Blue Lagoon.* Romantic stuff, you'd like it.'

'And R rated, that's why you want to see it. Why don't we go to the club?'

'What's the point of that, you don't even drink.'

Jenny wondered what was the point of going to the drive-in, when they never watched the movie, but she didn't say it. Her fingers toyed with a dandelion, clinging to life in the baked earth. 'You do love me, don't you, Tony?'

He tried to keep the exasperation out of his voice. 'Hey. How many times do I have to say it? You want me to come to the doctor's with you on Monday?'

'That'd be nice. I told him we were going to get married. We are, aren't we?'

'Sure. When I'm twenty-one.' When you're eighteen, three years is a lifetime away. Jenny, however, felt reassured.

'I just wish Dad understood.'

But Tony was in no mood for a deep and meaningful.

He sat up and grabbed her hand. 'Come on.'

'What?'

'Let's get into the van.'

'Now?'

'Why not now? You'll be on the pill on Monday. If we love each other, what's stopping us?' He tried to pull her up.

'Tony, no! It doesn't work like that!'

'What?'

'The pill. After I start taking it, we have to wait a month.' Tony knew next to nothing about contraception and this was news indeed; bad news. He felt foolish as well as angry. He jerked his towel out from under her. His voice was harsh.

'You know what you are Jenny? You're just a cockteaser.'

He stormed off towards the van, leaving Jenny shocked and bewildered. They'd had rows before but he had never spoken to her like that.

At the hospital Marta Kurtesz had received Frank's radio call with news of a motor vehicle accident at Five Mile Creek. He did not name the victims; he merely told her their condition, as far as Dr Bowen could ascertain, and the almost certain need for the operating theatre. Marta immediately rang the surgery and warned Shirley that Terence would be needed and possibly Shirley herself, while simultaneously giving instructions to Brendan to double-check the theatre and the resuscitation equipment, and to Judy to check their supplies of uncrossmatched blood and replacement fluid.

'Do we know who it is, Marta?'

'Sorry, Shirley. No idea at this stage.'

'Terence is on his way. I'll cancel all appointments here and follow him.'

She heard the ambulance passing. 'Did you hear that?

They'll be with you any minute. Let's hope it's not too bad.'

But when the ambos brought Elaine Mackay into the hospital's tiny emergency department, it was obvious straightaway that it was very bad indeed. Marta got a shock to see her friend lying on the gurney but she hid it well as she did the handover. Terence arrived almost as soon as the ambulance and conferred with Simon. They both agreed on the need to operate as soon as possible to discover the cause of the internal bleeding. She would probably need a transfusion. It was just assumed by everyone present that Terence would perform the surgery. Elaine was wheeled off to be prepped by Brendan but not before Marta had a quick word.

'You're okay with this?'

'Fine.'

'When I mentioned a baptism of fire …' She shook her head.

'We'll manage.' He gave her a quick smile and they were gone. Meanwhile, the ambos had brought Ian Sutton in. The head injury didn't appear to be serious but he did have multiple fractures. He'd been given morphine. He would have to wait until Elaine had been attended to.

Shirley Dean came hurrying in. 'What's the situation, can I help?'

Marta took her aside. 'Shirley, it's Elaine Mackay. And yes, we will need you.'

Shirley caught her breath. 'It's bad then?'

'Very.' They exchanged a long look. Elaine was someone they loved, someone they'd laughed with just that morning, she was not just another patient. But for the moment she had to be exactly that.

'Do we know how it happened?'

A grim-faced Frank Gilroy almost frog-marched Peter

Gleeson to a chair. 'Ask him!'

'Hang on!'

'Just sit there, Gleeson, and don't move.'

'I need medical attention.'

Frank ignored him and turned to Marta. 'I want a blood alcohol test on him.'

'I'll get Nurse Hammond to do it.' Frank nodded and went straight into her office. He knew where the relevant forms were. Marta let him be and turned to Shirley. 'Maybe you could look after Ian Sutton?'

'Ian?'

'He was in the car with Elaine.'

'How very odd. I assumed the other passenger was Andy.'

'We all did. Maybe Ian just gave her a lift somewhere. Here are the notes from the ambulance. Simon couldn't do much but give him morphine, he was too busy with Elaine.'

Frank returned. 'We didn't even have time to breathalyse this one.' He thrust the paper and a pen at Peter.

'Sign here.'

'What is it?'

'Sign it.'

Something in Frank's tone made Peter sign, however unwillingly. He hugged his chest and whimpered. Frank put the form in front of Shirley. 'Need a witness, please.'

'You'll need a doctor's order –'

'You'll get it, won't you, matron?'

Marta just nodded. 'Thank you,' said Frank and left. Shirley was dumbfounded. 'I don't think I've ever seen him like that.'

'Just doing his job.' Marta shook her head. 'Such a mess, Shirley …'

And it was going to get a whole lot messier.

***

Vicky had spent far more time at what was now most definitely the Jones' place than she had ever intended. She had decided she liked Molly who, while she might be more than a little mad, had a lot of courage in taking the farm on at all. And her enthusiasm was infectious. They were just finishing the grand tour and Molly was explaining how for her and Brendan it was like starting over; to have all this space, it was something they had talked of and dreamed of for years. That crowded, nine-to-five city life, with the pollution, the commuting, the rushing to and fro – it wasn't for them. They wanted a place where you could *breathe*. Sit and watch the grass grow.

Vicky laughed. 'I'll have to introduce you to Simon Bowen,' she said.

'Who?'

'Dr. Simon Bowen. Your Brendan may have met him already. He thinks this place is hicksville.'

'Oh. Hanging around, is he?'

Vicky grinned. 'Making his presence felt. Well, I should be off.'

'Just one more thing – do you think a goat would be practical? I love goats.'

'If you want to be self-sufficient then a cow would really make more sense. And once you start getting into livestock, then you'll need to think about forage crops.'

'You mean oats, barley ...? Stuff to make hay like lucerne?'

'All of the above.'

'I like the idea of haymaking. Sounds like fun.'

'There speaks a woman who has never done it.'

Vicky departed soon after, leaving a much brighter Molly behind her. Doris's glare, when she passed, seemed less-pronounced, the dunny appeared, by some optical illusion, to have straightened up a little and Molly felt that this new world she had so recently arrived in and which earlier had been so decidedly out of kilter, was now back on its axis and spinning serenely through a blue and sunlit space. Molly was never one to stay down for long.

Out at Five Mile Creek, Frank Gilroy was doing his job with his usual thoroughness. He may not have been a brilliant cop but he was a good one; determined and methodical, a bit of a terrier, he did not give up easily. While the tow-truck driver got Ian Sutton's vehicle hooked up, Frank measured skid marks and made notes and shook his head over the signs, which were exactly as he had feared and suspected. He recovered the three full beer cans from Peter Gleeson's Monaro and put them in a plastic bag. He found another, half-empty can on the floor with beer trickling out of it, poured out the dregs and put that in the bag also. He suspected that the two missing cans would be littering the road somewhere, Gleeson was not the sort of kid to be involved in any 'Keep Australia Beautiful' campaign.

He moved over to Ian's car and did a quick search, removing Elaine Mackay's handbag from the front seat. He was almost done when something shiny lying on the floor attracted his attention. He picked it up and looked at it thoughtfully. It was Elaine's wedding ring. He read the inscription on the inside of the band and then dropped it into his shirt pocket and waved to the tow-truck driver that he was done.

Vicky, unaware of how much she had played the good Samaritan at the Joneses' farm, visited a couple of clients then drove back into town. She was hungry so she stopped at the bakery for one of Andy Mackay's pies, settling, after much deliberation, on the chicken and leek.

'Did you hear the siren?' she asked Andy while he took the pie from the oven and put it in a bag.

'Yes, I did. Any idea what it was?' Vicky shook her head and gave him some money. 'Oh well, I guess it won't take long. Bad news travels fast, unfortunately.'

'Especially around here. Thanks, Andy.'

'See you, Vicky. Enjoy your pie.'

As Vicky got into her car, she saw the tow-truck go by, with a smashed-up station wagon on the back of it. Clearly readable on the side of the wagon was the wording 'Sutton's Stock Feed Eugowra'. Vicky did a double take. It was Ian Sutton's car. And Ian was a mate of Andy Mackay's. She wondered if Andy had seen it through the bakery window but thought that unlikely. She wondered if she should go back and tell him. She couldn't bring herself to do it. Hadn't they both just agreed that bad news travelled fast?

Elaine Mackay now lay close to death in the operating theatre which she had laboured so mightily to fill with the very latest and best equipment that a small country hospital could hope to possess. Capped and gowned, Terence, Simon, Marta and Brendan moved around her. There was little sound but the too-rapid beep of the cardiac monitor. Brendan connected a new bag of blood to the drip; Simon adjusted the anaesthetic tube down Elaine's throat; Marta swabbed her abdomen. Terence asked about Elaine's vital signs.

Marta responded that her blood pressure was low and dropping, her pulse was high, weak and thready. They all knew there was not a moment to lose. Terence asked for a scalpel which Marta handed him. He turned to Simon.

'Ready?'

'I need fifteen seconds.'

Terence nodded and silently hoped they had fifteen seconds. To fill the time, he told Marta unnecessarily to be ready with the sucker as soon as he went in.

Finally, Simon said he was ready and Terence made a swift incision. Marta was ready with the sucker and swabs. Terence worked away. There was blood everywhere, he couldn't see what he was doing for it. He asked for more suction, it just wasn't working.

Simon asked, 'Where's it coming from, the spleen?'

Terence shook his head, he didn't know. 'I can't see.'

Simon asked Brendan for more pressure and Brendan pumped up the airbag surrounding the plastic bag of blood while Marta swabbed away with packs and applied suction as hard as she could. Still the blood came. Trying to keep his voice even, Simon announced that Elaine's blood pressure was dropping.

'Nearly there,' Terence said. 'Very nearly –' Then he froze. 'Good God, it's the aorta.'

Simon looked despairingly at the blood pressure read-out. 'Nothing we can do.' But Terence wasn't ready to give up.

'I'll try a repair,' he said, even though he – all of them – knew it was hopeless. 'Keep the blood going in.'

They went on working, putting up blood, preparing sutures, fighting for Elaine against all the odds.

CHAPTER FOURTEEN

It has to be said that no-one was doing a great deal for Peter Gleeson. Shirley and Judy Loveday had attended to Ian Sutton, doing what they could to stabilise him until the theatre was free. His skull had been x-rayed and his left leg, broken in two places, strapped to the right one. He'd also been given more pain relief.

Meanwhile, Peter was still sitting on the chair where Frank Gilroy had dumped him. Ruth Hammond had taken the blood sample and packed it ready to go to Burrigan for testing but no one had had the time to do much else, it was a simple matter of triage – not victimisation, as Peter himself kept insisting. But when he started coughing up blood, Judy was quickly at his side. 'I told you I was crook,' he said.

'We'll get an x-ray done and see what's going on.'

Peter felt vindicated. 'It hurts like hell.'

'Yeah, well that's broken ribs for you. But they do mend.'

Shirley offered to organise the x-ray. 'Pneumothorax, do you think?'

'Could be, Shirl. Better not take any chances with the little sod.' Judy, as usual, had already rushed to judgement but fortunately Peter did not hear that little aside. It was then that Brendan, still in his theatre gown, stuck his head into emergency.

'Can't come in, I'm sterile, but we need more blood. A positive.'

'Right you are.' Judy was on to it.

'Hey, what about me!' from Peter.

Shirley hadn't met Brendan yet but she was looking to him for answers. 'What is it?'

'Ruptured aorta.'

'Oh, dear God.' And seeing her reaction, Peter Gleeson shut up and for a moment kept his troubles to himself.

Bob Hatfield, who'd lived in Wandin Valley all his life, arrived on Molly Jones' doorstep just as the removal van was departing and found her surrounded by still more boxes and a quantity of furniture clearly in excess of requirements for the small house. He removed his hat and introduced himself, and Molly's small hand disappeared into a giant paw.

'Bob Hatfield, Wandin Valley Pump Company. And you're Molly Jones.'

Molly agreed that indeed she was and refrained from asking how he knew. This was the country, she assumed that by now everyone knew. They appraised each other. Molly saw a big, smiling man with prematurely white hair and a ruddy face. He was dressed in King Gees and a checked shirt and work boots, he couldn't have been more country if he'd been chewing on a hay straw. Bob took in the leotard, the sloppy joe, the glittered gum boots and thought, God help us, had she run away from a circus? But he just asked if maybe she was about to go out somewhere (he did not suggest a fancy-dress party), he could always come back. Molly reassured him about her taste for bright clothes.

'It makes me feel happy,' she said. 'Positive, you know? Though I'm not sure Doris approves.'

'Oh, don't let Doris get to you, love, she's a cantankerous old so-and-so.'

Molly warmed to Bob immediately. 'Oh, you know her, do you?'

'Do I ever. I'll let you into a little secret, Molly. If she ever gets really difficult, give her a bottle of beer. Calms her down right away.'

'Beer?'

'Beer. Old Davo did that and it worked a treat.'

'I'll remember.'

'Whereas your generator now … which has a temperament not unlike Doris's … if that gives you trouble you're better off calling me.'

'Oh, I see. Well the thing is, Brendan and me – Brendan's my husband –'

'Doctor, right?'

'Nurse, actually.'

'Nurse? Really?' Bob was thinking it certainly did take all types.

'The thing is,' Molly went on, 'we really want to be self-sufficient as much as we can. Do everything for ourselves.'

'Independent. Good idea. Save a heap of money too. All the same – if the genny ever gets too much –'

'Wandin Valley Pump.'

'I'm in the book. Well. You got plenty to keep you busy, I won't hold you up. Unless you need a hand with anything?' He waved at the boxes.

'Thanks but –'

'Independent.'

'It's not that,' said Molly. 'It's just that I haven't a clue where to begin.'

'Moving,' Bob said. 'I tried it once. Well. Nice to meet you, Molly Jones.'

She thanked him for the tip about Doris and as he got back into his truck, asked him about the ambulance siren. Bob's smile faded. 'Country roads. Got to be careful, love. All the time. Remember that.'

Back in the theatre, Terence wanted aortic clamps but that was one bit of equipment they didn't have. He made do with the covered bowel clamps Marta offered him instead, working feverishly to get at the damaged aorta.

'Sixteen minutes,' he said.

'Counting down.'

Brendan checked the time on his watch. They all knew that if the clamps stayed on any longer than that, Elaine could end up a paraplegic. Terence was sweating profusely; the stress in the usually calm theatre was palpable. Simon tersely announced that Elaine's blood pressure was still dropping. Brendan moved to change the bags.

Simon expressed concern about Elaine's kidneys and then Brendan had more bad news.

'This is the last blood,' he said. 'We have two plasma and that's it.'

Simon asked if they had Hartmann's solution and Marta answered in the affirmative. Simon breathed again but only momentarily.

'Damn, it's breaking away!' Terence's repair wasn't holding. 'More packs. And another suture. 4/0 polypropylene. We'll try again.'

Simon shook his head. 'I can't maintain the blood pressure.'

'Well pump faster!'

'Fourteen minutes.' Brendan announced, loud and clear, as the heartbeat monitor gave a couple of small hiccups.

'Heartbeat's irregular.' Simon did not enjoy being the bearer of bad news.

Terence chose to ignore it anyway and tried once more to suture the aorta. 'Just keep her alive,' he said.

Sandra Myers knew something was going on in the hospital but she wasn't sure what. She'd pressed her buzzer a couple of times and no one had come but she didn't really mind. She felt worn out, physically and emotionally and she was quite happy to lie there and do nothing. She was glad no one had come to pressure her to make decisions because in truth she felt incapable of making them. Her life had come to a crossroads, but where it would go from here was a big unknown. She was a little surprised that Bernie hadn't turned up and tried to drag her away; maybe he'd already gone back to Lynette. She tried to banish that thought, it made her want to cry again though she did not understand why it should. Perhaps she just couldn't bear the thought of him being happy when she herself was so miserable.

Judy Loveday was right about one thing. Sandra Myers *had* been spoilt, in the sense that life had never, until now, asked much of her in the way of suffering or hardship; little harm had been shown her and consequently, the art of forgiveness was not something she'd had to learn. The question was whether she could learn it in time to be a mother to her baby. She saw Nurse Hammond pass her door and called her; and Ruth, who was a country girl and didn't have much time for the Sandras of this world, stuck her head in.

'Yes, Mrs Myers, what is it?'

'I just wondered what was happening.'

'If you're not getting much attention it's because we're very busy. There's been a terrible car accident.'

'Oh, that's awful. Are they local people?'

Hammond, who was upset, just said yes, they were.

'I'm so sorry. I'm fine. Don't worry, I don't need a thing.'

Hammond just nodded and hurried off. Sandra saw a man in police uniform also pass along the corridor. She lay there and thought how close she had come to having an accident herself and felt a twinge of gratitude for the first time since she'd arrived in Wandin Valley.

Sometimes, in an operating theatre, a good outcome is all but guaranteed. The team is there to achieve a known end, to save a life or improve its quality, sometimes to a remarkable degree. Then it is a job like few others, with enormous satisfaction shared by all involved. At other times, no amount of training and experience, of effort and dedication, seem able to produce the hoped for result. This was such a time. Simon Bowen thought a miracle was needed and Wandin Valley, it appeared, was on by-pass for miracles. He stared at the heart monitor next to him and listened to its erratic pips. He said aloud, 'The xylocard's not having any effect.'

'Last one.' As Terence concluded his feverish stitching the pips stopped altogether. The monitor made a flat, continuous tone.

'Asystole,' said Simon. Elaine's heart had stopped beating.

Terence stepped back, Simon and Brendan had the paddles on Elaine's chest in a moment, the charge went through and her body contorted. Her heart beat briefly and died once more. They were about to use the paddles again when Marta stopped them, pointing out renewed bleeding. Terence was finding it hard to accept that his repair had failed a second time. He demanded more sutures, he would try again. Simon hesitated, he knew Elaine was beyond help but he understood Terence's very real anguish. It was Marta who finally stepped in.

'Terence,' she said, 'it's finished.'

He turned to argue but she looked at him steadily and he gave in. It was indeed over. There would be no miracle this time.

All signs of that Herculean medical effort were removed. With care and respect, Elaine Mackay's body was returned to something approaching normality, and removed to await her loved ones. Shirley heard the awful news from Terence and Marta. She was shocked but then they'd been so long in theatre, she was half-expecting it, had been steeling herself for the worst. She'd been trying to ring Andy ... she'd try again. It really hit her then, she felt a bit faint and she left them to deal with Ian Sutton, once the theatre was ready, and went off for a moment by herself.

Peter Gleeson had been admitted to a ward and that was where Frank Gilroy found him. He walked in unannounced, pulled a chair up close to Peter's bed and took out a notebook. 'A few questions.'

'It hurts to talk,' Peter said. 'I've got a collapsed lung.'

'I checked with the medical staff. They said it was okay. What pub were you drinking at?'

Peter denied having been at any pub at all but Frank wasn't buying it. Not when the publican at the Royal had Peter drinking there at opening time. Peter admitted to two beers. Frank pointed out, quite patiently, that the blood test would tell them how many. Peter had also bought a six-pack. Frank had found three unopened in the car. What of the others?

Peter decided that silence was golden.

'I warned you, Gleeson – was it only two days ago? Watch yourself, stay out of trouble, you and those no-hopers you hang out with. And now this.' He sighed deeply. 'So how fast were you going?'

'I heard what you said when you pulled me over. I

did! And I wasn't speeding!'

About then, Frank's patience began to run out. 'Listen to me, son. I measured your skid marks. Twenty-three metres! You took the bend too fast, it was either hit the bridge or hit Ian Sutton's car, so you went for the car, tried to squeeze through, thought you could get away with it.'

Peter was shaking his head but Frank took no notice. He tapped the notebook. 'That's what it says here. That's what you're going to sign.'

But Peter didn't sign, not then anyway, because Frank saw Shirley standing at the door and knew straightaway that something was very wrong. He told Peter that he'd be back and went out to her. Peter watched him go and waited. After a moment Judy Loveday came in. He thought she looked a bit red-eyed. She put a pill in front of him and poured water from his jug. Peter asked what had happened. She didn't reply, she just told him to take the pill. He demanded an answer.

Judy looked at him coldly. 'Elaine Mackay's dead. Something for you to think about.' It was not perhaps very professional but Judy didn't care. She left him to it.

In Marta's office, Frank was doing his best to comfort Shirley, he knew how close she and Elaine had been. Shirley was trying hard to maintain her composure and only just succeeding.

'I tried to get on to Andy but there was no answer … I can't imagine where he is. Those poor boys of theirs will have to be told …' She caught her breath, fighting to keep the tears at bay. 'Such a waste, Frank, a person like that, who worked all her life to help others. Why is it always the good people?'

And then, out of the blue, Andy Mackay appeared in the doorway and said hello and wondered what Frank and Shirley were doing there in the Matron's office? He said he'd heard the ambulance siren and then he'd seen

Ian Sutton's car, all smashed up on the back of the tow-truck and well, Ian was a really good friend, heaven's, Andy and Elaine were only talking about him this morning. Did they know if he was alright?

Frank saw a chance to do something for Shirley then and he explained, very calmly, that Ian was okay, he had a couple of fractures but the doctors were attending to him there and then. And he suggested to Andy that they go outside, there was something Frank needed to talk to him about and with all the experience of twenty years of policing behind him, twenty years of breaking the worst possible news, Frank gently ushered Andy away.

Shirley sat there for a while and it occurred to her that Frank Gilroy, for all his faults, was the salt of the earth. At last she did something she knew she would regret if it were left undone and she made her way to a small room near the morgue. In there, on a hospital trolley, was the covered body of her friend. She lifted the sheet back from Elaine's face and looked at her for a long time.

'Darling Elaine. Thank you for giving so much ...' She bent and kissed Elaine's forehead.

She was still there, sitting on a chair beside the trolley, when Frank brought a shattered Andy in to say goodbye to his wife. Shirley got up and gave him a silent hug and he clung to her for a few moments, knowing that she shared something of his grief, then she and Frank moved away to give him some privacy.

Andy looked down at his wife, almost as if he expected her to come back to life, to speak to him. He touched her cheek with the back of his hand, then brushed a wisp of hair off her face, as lovers do, and smiled at her, and wept. And then, after a while, he went back to Frank. 'I'll have to ring the school. The boys have to be told.'

'Why don't I take you home, Andy. We can do it there.'

'Home?'

'Come on, mate.' Once again, he put an arm around Andy. 'Will you be alright, Shirl?'

'Yes. There are things to do here, still.'

'I'll call you later.'

The two men left together. Shirley pulled the sheet back over Elaine's body and followed them out, closing the door behind her. Then, much as Elaine herself would have done, Shirley went to see where else she might be needed on this terrible day.

CHAPTER FIFTEEN

At Andy Mackay's house, Frank made strong tea and Andy phoned first his sister in Albury, who promised to come straightaway, and then the boys' boarding school. The house master would break the news and then they could ring their father. He offered his condolences and any help with travel arrangements. Andy spoke of them fondly to Frank, of how they adored their mother. He didn't know how they would cope with the loss but Frank said that children were often more resilient than we imagined.

Andy told Frank how Elaine had gone to see him in the bakery that morning. 'I wonder if she somehow knew? They say people do sometimes, a sort of premonition?'

'I don't know, Andy. Maybe.'

Andy sipped his tea.

'I suppose Ian gave her a lift.' Frank just nodded. Andy was upset that he hadn't been able to see Ian, who was still in theatre, but Frank, trying to deflect the conversation away from dangerous ground, said he could see Ian tomorrow, he wasn't going anywhere.

'How did it happen, Frank? I mean, whose fault was it?'

'We don't know that yet.'

'What, you mean it could be a court matter?'

'Possibly.'

'Well it wouldn't be Ian Sutton. He's on the road all the time and he's careful. Elaine always says – she used to say – he drove like an old woman. So who else was involved?'

So Frank was forced to give him the bare facts: that Peter Gleeson was driving his Monaro and that he'd suffered some minor injuries. He refused to be drawn on whether or not Peter had been drinking but the name was enough for Andy. Gleeson was a good-for-nothing, layabout dole-bludger who spent his government handout on getting plastered. And now he'd killed Andy's wife!

Frank could understand only too well that Andy, in his grief, needed someone to lash out at and Gleeson was just the candidate. Frank felt a burning anger towards the kid himself. But he wanted the matter to go forward as it should; he wanted Peter Gleeson to feel the full weight and majesty of the law, to be crushed by it in fact, and nothing must be allowed to hinder that process. He therefore did his best to calm Andy down and felt he had succeeded.

The surgery on Ian Sutton had finally been completed and he would soon be out of recovery and taken to a ward. Brendan had slipped out to call Molly and let her know he'd be late home. He was a little concerned about how she was coping. As he made his way to Marta's office he found Bernard Myers in the corridor, looking a bit lost. Bernard wanted to see his daughter and Brendan took him to the nursery. He cooed over the baby and then he asked about Sandra. Brendan explained about the day from hell and apologised that he wasn't able to tell Bernard much.

'Why don't you pop in and see her?' he said.

'Awkward,' said Bernie. 'She doesn't want to see me.'

'Oh, I see, I didn't know there was a problem. Sorry.' Bernie just shrugged it off. 'All the same, you'll have to talk sometime, the two of you. Got to make plans for this little one.'

'I know that. Only too well.'

It was then that Brendan, unaware that certain promises had been made, gave some very bad advice. 'You know what I think – not that it's any of my business? Sometimes you've just got to take the bull by the horns. Barge right in and hang the consequences.' It sounded like a plan to Bernard Myers.

A few minutes later, he knocked on Sandra's door and barged in. She spun around and saw him and was not pleased.

'Who said you could come in?'

'No one. I had to see you.'

'Well I don't want to see you. I want a divorce.' Not quite what Bernard was hoping for. He didn't respond. 'Well?'

'I had a speech prepared. Now I'm hurting too much to say anything.'

'*You're* hurting! You went back to her, Bernie! I was pregnant with your child and you went back to her! So take the child and go to her and stay there!'

'You don't mean that.'

'I mean every word.'

'I don't love her. I love you.'

'I saw you with her. The whole world saw you. On television. When you won with *my* design.'

'*We* won. And yes, I got drunk and I behaved like an

idiot. But it was us, you and me that did it. You wouldn't believe the orders we've got. Not just for the resort wear, for everything. Even bridal, I've had to put three extra girls on, just cutting, we're going to have our best year ever. And you know what? I don't even care. It won't mean a damn thing if you're not there.'

She didn't even look at him. The pain went too deep. He tried once more to get through to her.

'I don't know what to say. When I got home and you weren't there, I nearly went mad. I phoned hospitals, police, everyone and everywhere I could think of. I even phoned the morgue. I drove to Newcastle, in case you'd gone to Rosemary's ... I didn't know she was in London. I can't believe this is happening to us.'

What she said in reply seemed like a complete non sequitur. 'This hospital has been full of sadness today. Someone died. Someone that everyone loved.'

'Yes. Yes, I know. A car accident. I was so afraid that's what had happened to you.'

'It nearly did. Would you leave now, please?'

'What about the baby? Have you even seen her?' But Sandra had turned away.

Bernard left his wife then and stumbled out into the corridor and walked towards the main entrance. He thought of snatching the baby and going away forever but such drastic action seemed ridiculous, like something out of a film. He passed Marta's office. She was there with Brendan and Terence and Simon. He paused in the doorway.

He looked at Brendan. 'It didn't work.' To them all he said, 'She won't have me back and she doesn't want the baby. I don't know what I'm supposed to do. I know it's my fault but I can't see that slashing my wrists will help. Maybe I should just find a solicitor.'

Marta tried to console him. She said they would try to come up with something, that Sandra wasn't quite rational, she'd been through a lot and she needed time. Bernard should come back tomorrow. Terence agreed.

Not much comforted, Bernard left. Marta looked at the men. 'Any suggestions?'

Brendan backed off. 'I think I've done enough damage,' he said. 'I'll go and check on Miss Bird for penance.'

Terence and Simon decided to consider the options over a well-earned drink. They did not, as anyone else might have done, head for the pub. As Terence knew and Simon was learning, in a small community the local doctor was under constant scrutiny; more than a single glass of wine with a meal was likely to set tongues wagging. So they went to back to Terence's flat where he opened a rather nice Hunter Valley shiraz and produced some food which they barely touched. It was Elaine they talked of first, or rather Simon did. He was still very new to it all, still perhaps half believing that as doctors they could save everyone. He'd gone over and over it in his mind, he said, he didn't think there was anything more they could have done. Unless, perhaps, they'd been at a big city hospital, the Royal North Shore or St Vincent's, somewhere like that, where they could have got their hands on a Teflon graft ... Terence made no contribution.

'If we could have got to her quicker,' Simon said. 'Maybe time was the thing. If we'd got her on the table sooner.' Again he looked to Terence for confirmation but it wasn't forthcoming.

'Simon, you said it before. We did everything we could. We're not in the business of performing miracles, though heaven knows we try. Really, Elaine was dead the minute the car left the road. Her aorta was severely ruptured, we tried to repair it but we couldn't. End of story.'

Simon stared into his glass for a long time. 'I'm sorry.

I'll get used to it, I suppose. In time.'

'Yes,' said Terence. 'You will. But it's always going to be harder here in the country, because so often it's someone you know and like.'

Simon nodded. 'Even I knew Elaine and I've only been here a few months. They've got kids, haven't they, boys?'

'Yes.'

'The damage that drunken lout has done.'

'You don't know he was drunk.'

'He stank of it, Terence. At that time of day!'

Terence didn't want to go there. 'I thought Brendan Jones did well.'

'Yeah. Seems like a nice guy too. Empathetic, that's the word.' They chatted for a while longer and then Simon, getting the sense that Terence wanted to be alone, reluctantly went off home to his very unwelcoming unit at the pub.

After her encounter with Tony at the waterhole, Jenny had ridden back to the farm by the slowest route possible, waved to her father who, thank goodness, was ploughing in the bottom paddock, and disappeared into her bedroom. When, much later, Hal poked his head in she pretended to be doing homework and indeed there were books scattered around but nothing could have been further from her mind. She had spent the time worrying about her relationship with Tony, whom she still loved in spite of the way he'd behaved. She tried to make excuses for him. She knew he was disappointed because she understood how boys were, like small children who expected to get what they wanted, but deep down she also knew that he'd treated her badly and she was hurt. The question was, where did she go from here? She wanted the situation resolved; she wanted to be grown up about it and she did not want to lose him. How to achieve all that she had no idea and no one to ask for advice.

Hal wanted to know if she was going out, it being Saturday night, and was surprised to learn that she wasn't. He wondered if she'd be alright alone at home and she got annoyed, of course she would, she'd done it before.

And then, before she could stop herself, because she hated her life right then, she said, 'Or don't you trust me, is that it? You think I'm going to get Tony round, have it off with him in my bedroom?'

Somehow – perhaps because he sensed that all was not right with Jenny's world – Hal managed to ignore that. He just said he was going to the club with a friend, it would be a quiet night and an early one, no one was in the mood for partying on after what had happened today. And at least they agreed about that.

'You can get yourself something to eat then?'

She just gave him a look and he had the grace to admit it was a pretty dumb question. She'd been doing most of the cooking since Penny died. He wondered why he didn't tell her he was going with Vicky Dean; silly, but he had an odd little feeling she wouldn't approve.

Vicky herself felt odd about going out, on this of all nights, as though it showed a lack of proper feeling. Though she suspected that Elaine, were she there, would have encouraged her to go, and Shirley too for that matter.

'I hate leaving you here by yourself. After the day you've had.'

'I won't be by myself. Frank's coming round to cook me dinner.'

'Frank is?'

'Yes, well he knew I wouldn't feel like going to the club but he said I had to eat. And I suppose he's right.

Not that I feel like it.'

'He's very thoughtful, Mum.' She meant it.

'I know, I know. I'll still have to tell him he's not for me.'

'Is this the right time?'

'Yes it is. Just because he *is* so thoughtful and kind, I can't lead him on, can I? You go, darling – try to enjoy yourself.'

Vicky left her behind with some apprehension. She felt she would probably spend the night fretting over what was happening between her mother and the good sergeant Gilroy, rather than paying attention to Hal Secombe.

An exhausted Marta was still at the hospital, finishing off some paperwork. If only they had an administrator she thought, for the umpteenth time that week, she might have a life. She signed a last form, then picked up the phone. It was Terence who answered; Terence, who'd been drinking malt whisky ever since the door closed behind Simon.

'How are you?'

Terence smiled at the concern in her voice. 'Not too bad, young Dr Bowen stayed for quite a while. I had to keep myself tidy.'

'I was worried,' Marta said. 'You fought so hard for Elaine.'

'I spent some time telling Simon that we can't perform miracles.'

'You do believe that?'

'Yes. But it doesn't stop you hoping, does it? I admit there was a moment when I thought, if I could save her, it might balance things somehow ...'

'She was dead from the moment those two cars collided, Terence.'

'I said that to Simon as well.'

'Then please, just accept it.'

'I'm trying. The whisky helps.'

'Don't drink too much.'

'No. Not too much. And Marta – thank you.'

'Anytime.' She hung up.

Terence sat down with his glass and swirled the golden liquid around for a long time before he took another sip. In her office, Marta shook her head, only slightly less concerned. Then she was startled to see Andy Mackay walk past her doorway. She quickly followed him.

'Mr Mackay! Can I help you?' At first he ignored her but she called again and without turning he said, with a wild note to his voice, that he was going to see Peter Gleeson.

Marta told him that wasn't possible, visiting hours were over but Andy ignored her and kept going, peering into every room, shouting for Gleeson. Peter heard him coming and managed to get out of bed just as Andy reached the door. Marta was glad to see Brendan appear from Miss Bird's room and the two of them rushed in behind Andy. Peter Gleeson cowered on the other side of the bed, pulling the visitor's chair in front of him. He looked like a terrified child.

'Mr Mackay, please, you must come with us,' Marta demanded quietly. 'You must stop this, it is not going to help.'

But Andy was quite mad with grief, he'd had hours now to think about his loss, to realise that his adored Elaine was gone forever, and someone had to pay. He pointed a finger at Peter, frozen behind the chair. 'You killed my wife. And you're not going to get away with it, Gleeson, I swear to God you're not!'

Brendan put firm arms around Andy. 'Come on, mate. We all know how you feel. But this isn't the time or the place. Come on.' He went on talking, low and calm, and eventually anger gave way to grief and Andy let Brendan lead him away.

Marta ordered Peter back into bed, her tone a little more brusque than usual. Peter felt the atmosphere and resented it.

'The guy's mad.'

'Grief does that to people. You'll understand when you grow up. Now lie there quietly or you'll do yourself more damage.'

'I dunno why everyone's got it in for me. It wasn't my fault. Sutton was on the wrong side of the road.'

Marta explained that the rights and wrongs of it were not her province, told him to ring if he needed painkillers and left him to it.

Brendan found her back in her office, after he'd seen a subdued and slightly embarrassed Andy to his car. 'I don't know what got into me,' he'd said to Brendan. 'Suddenly it all just came over me, you know? How *wrong* it was. The boys'll be home tomorrow – what am I going to tell them?'

'And what is he going to tell them, Matron?' Brendan said now to Marta. 'I'm damned if I know. The usual platitudes about how much their mother loved them?'

'She adored them. She'd have given her life for them. It has to mean something.'

'I suppose so.'

Marta managed a smile.

'Go home to your wife, Mr Jones. You've been a tower of strength today, I don't know what we would have done without you.'

'It was – busy.' He smiled. 'Can I be Brendan, please.'

'Of course.'

'One last thing. Dr Elliott.'

'You're going to say: he's not just a GP, is he?'

'And you'd rather I didn't ask.'

'If you don't mind.'

'He did a fantastic job, whatever he is. Night, Matron.'

'Goodnight, Brendan.'

CHAPTER SIXTEEN

By the time Molly saw the station wagon turn off the Tallebung Road and into their own drive, she was more than a little tired. Apart from her two visitors, she'd dealt with a truckload of household goods, a constantly failing generator and a totally recalcitrant pig. Of these, Doris had caused by far the most pain; it wasn't just her baleful gaze, or the fact that she had deliberately (Molly was sure it was deliberate) upended her dinner all over Molly's most glittery gumboots. It was her insouciance, her air of having the upper hand, of knowing that Molly *knew* she had the upper hand and positively wallowing in the knowledge. Molly was beginning to harbour less than charitable feelings towards Doris.

Nevertheless, while Brendan had not said a lot in his earlier phone call, Molly had picked up enough to realise that it hadn't been the best of days at Wandin Valley Hospital. She was therefore determined to put a good face on things and greeted him with a hug, and since the evening was still warm they sat on the verandah nursing a couple of beers.

'So how was it?' Molly wanted to know and Brendan, glad to have someone to unload it all on, told her. Told her about the much-loved woman who had died and about the young man whom everyone suspected was to blame – already the grieving husband had attacked him and the police sergeant was out to get him and if he *were* responsible then his life too would be ruined. He told her about the injured best friend and the country GP with the skills of a top-flight surgeon and strange Miss Bird, Queen of the Drovers, and finally about poor little rich girl, Sandra Myers, who had to learn how to forgive and forget or there'd be three kids made motherless in Wandin Valley instead of two.

Molly listened to him and realised again how much she loved him, because he really cared about these people whom he'd only known for a minute, and she thought she could probably cope with Doris, though possibly not the dunny, but she'd leave that till the morning. Brendan put an arm around her and asked about her day and she just smiled and said she'd met some amazing people as well. And they both agreed they'd come to a good place, if first impressions were anything to go by.

This longest of days was still far from over. Frank had cooked Shirley a simple meal, a chicken breast poached in white wine with baby potatoes and some sautéed spinach. He would have liked to impress her with something a little more flashy but guessed, correctly, that she would barely know what she was eating and nutrition was all that really mattered. Shirley herself was in an absolute state. Added to her grief over Elaine was the knowledge that she was going to have to hurt this very kind man. She drank far too much as she tried to find the gentlest way to do it.

Frank, for his part, had a dilemma of his own. On the

one hand, he wanted to keep Shirley's mind off the distressing events of the day. On the other, he needed advice about the wedding ring that was burning a hole in his pocket and she, as one of Elaine's closest friends, was the person to give it. Perhaps it could wait till tomorrow. He cleared the table, refusing her offer to help.

'Lovely meal, Frank.'

'Thanks, Shirl. But we'll still go to the club, as soon as you're feeling up to it.' He carefully skirted the pyramid as he brought out the dessert. He asked her if she really sat under it and meditated. She assured him she most certainly did. He looked nonplussed and admitted that he'd thought Vicky was joking.

Shirley suggested he try it some time.

'I don't think so, Shirl.'

'But it's so relaxing.'

'I think I'll stick with growing roses.'

Shirley managed a little laugh. 'Well, each to his own. We're very different, you and I.'

'Oh absolutely. You were always a bit eccentric, that's what I like about you.'

Shirley took a deep breath. 'Frank. Can we talk seriously for a minute?'

'Well of course, Shirl. There's things we need to discuss. But only if you feel up to it. I don't want you getting upset.'

Shirley was puzzled. She thought it was Frank who'd be getting upset. She ploughed on. 'It's just that I don't think us going to the club together is such a good idea after all.'

It was Frank's turn to be puzzled. 'Why ever not?'

'I don't see the point in starting something we can't continue. Not without someone getting hurt.'

'Doesn't Vicky approve?'

'It's got nothing to do with Vicky!'

'Oh. Then who could get hurt?'

Shirley spelled it out as gently as she could. 'Frank, what I'm trying to say is that you're a lovely bloke but you're just not my type.'

He was hurt. Shirley could see that he was hurt. It wasn't what she wanted, not on this of all nights. She tried to take all the blame by pointing out that it wasn't him, it was her. She didn't want to be involved with anyone. She was too selfish, too much of a nutcase, she'd drive any man mad who had to live with her. She not only sat under a pyramid, she believed in spirits, she read tea leaves.

Frank took all this in and to her consternation said he didn't have a problem with it. Shirley played her last card.

'And I smoke grass,' she said. Frank looked puzzled again. She elaborated. 'Pot. Marihuana. I love it. Are you going to arrest me?'

There was a long pause. 'You don't really, do you?' Frank asked.

Shirley couldn't lie to him. She sighed. 'No. But I might. One day I definitely might. You need someone more stable than me, Frank. Someone respectable. Pillar of the community. Like – I don't know.'

He thought she probably had Elaine in mind. He didn't want to disillusion her. He really didn't think she knew what she was saying, she wasn't herself at all. He was sure they could still work things out.

'Tell you what, Shirl. Been a hell of a day. Let's leave it for now. There's something I need your help with, how about I come and see you first thing tomorrow, would that be okay?'

Shirley had no choice but to agree. It was as well that she had no idea what he was talking about, or it would have kept her awake all night.

***

Vicky and Hal had not stayed long at the club. Their meal wasn't too bad, considering the chef was away on sick leave, and the band had done their best and chosen their numbers with sensitivity. Nevertheless, it was one of those nights when everyone should have stayed at home and stared at the telly. Because everyone was acutely aware of what had happened that day and all of them, to greater or lesser extent, were affected by it. Normal chat proved difficult and laughter felt out of place; Vicky was worried about Shirley and Hal even more so about Jenny so they bonded by sharing their concerns and found that they enjoyed each other's company very much.

They wouldn't have minded, either of them, if they had found something more; they were exploring the possibility with a gentle kiss back in Hal's kitchen. It didn't really happen; no violins, no fireworks, nothing like the movies – and ruined, in any case, by the entrance of Jenny. Vicky and Hal separated without any real embarrassment but Jenny was in the mood to lash out.

'Sorry! Didn't mean to interrupt!'

'Hi, Jenny,' Vicky smiled. Jenny ignored her and turned to Hal.

'Of course it's alright for you, I bet *she's* on the pill!' And she fled back to her room.

'Oh dear.' Vicky shook her head. 'Maybe our timing wasn't the best.'

Hal was mortified that his daughter could be so rude but Vicky laughed it off, she felt sorry for Jenny who was clearly suffering the sort of angst that only teenagers had to endure.

'Trouble in paradise?' she asked Hal.

'I honestly don't know. She wasn't very happy when she came home. Maybe they've had a row.'

'And you wouldn't be mean enough to hope it lasts,

would you, Hal?' It was too close to the bone for Hal to laugh. Vicky thought, given that he'd be up milking at five, that it was time she left. Hal walked her out to her car. It was one of those hot, clear nights when the stars glittered so brightly they seemed almost within reach, a night for lovers, Vicky thought.

'Fantastic, isn't it?' Hal was looking up at the heavens too.

Vicky nodded. 'It makes you glad to be alive.' She hesitated. 'I hope Andy's okay.'

'Yeah.'

'I'm sorry. This must all bring back memories.'

'You never get over it. You move on, that's all.'

Vicky gave Hal a little hug and thanked him for a pleasant evening. They didn't kiss again; they both seemed to feel that a friendship might be more important than anything else.

After Vicky had driven away, Hal stood looking at the sky for a long time. Then he went inside, washed the coffee cups and, on his way to bed, stopped to tap on Jenny's closed door.

'Jen? You alright?'

'Fine.'

He knew she was anything but fine but he didn't push it. Like many others in Wandin Valley, Hal Secombe went off to a restless night, haunted by dreams from the past, filled with worries about the daughter he loved.

Shirley was still up when Vicky got in and glad to have someone to talk to about her rather puzzling evening. 'I'm glad you're home early, how did it go?'

'Yeah, nice. I mean, Hal's nice. But the atmosphere at the club ...' She shook her head. 'Not the best night to go. What about you and the good sergeant?'

'Totally weird.' And Shirley explained how Frank cooked her a very nice meal but seemed to think the vast differences in their personalities were no hindrance at all to a relationship between them. 'I really think he believes he can still win me around.'

Vicky had to smile. 'Maybe he can.'

'He has no hope! None. Zilch.'

'Whatever you say, Mum.'

'Whose side are you on?'

'I'm not taking sides! I'm too tired.'

'Hell of a day.'

'Yep.'

'So – you and Hal?'

'No. But he's a really good bloke.'

'Simon will be pleased.'

'Don't you say a word to Simon!' Vicky got up. 'Bedtime. Do you think you'll be able to sleep?'

Shirley shook her head. 'Frank said he needs my help with something tomorrow. He sounded serious. I can't imagine what it is.' She sat there worrying about it. Vicky decided to make her some camomile tea. She thought her mother quite possibly needed something stronger than the leaves of a little flower to relieve the pain she was feeling but it couldn't do any harm.

CHAPTER SEVENTEEN

In the pre-dawn light, Andy Mackay found himself in his bakery, about to light the ovens. He was on automatic pilot, he had no idea how he had even got there. He looked around and actually thought about getting to work, he had a vague idea that the familiar smell of flour and yeast might offer some sort of comfort, that the work itself would take his mind off things. Then he realised how foolish it was. Nothing would relieve the torment he was going through.

The whole business was still incomprehensible, the fact that Elaine was in the car with Ian in the first place, that she'd got a lift with him somewhere, why he couldn't imagine, and then for Peter Gleeson to run them off the road ... he'd see Ian later, maybe he could explain it, or some of it.

A woman came into the bakery, for a crazy moment he thought it was her, Elaine, bringing coffee like she did yesterday, but it wasn't Elaine. It was Margie, his sister, urging him to come back to the house, they wouldn't be opening today, come and try to get some more sleep. And because she meant well and he was too tired to argue, he did as she asked.

The sun rose some hours later and soon warmed the corrugated iron of the Joneses' outdoor dunny, where Molly had taken herself to attend to the call of nature before Brendan should disappear down the drive again. It was fortuitous that his shift did not start too early. Molly was enthroned in peaceful contemplation, listening to the dawn chorus and also to the snuffles and gruntles of Doris in her pen not far away. She was thinking that if she perhaps painted the pen in a bright but soothing shade it might put Doris in a better humour. She was going through the colour spectrum in her mind and had almost settled on a nice, warm peach when a tiny movement over the doorway of the dunny caught her eye. A large, hairy huntsman waved a leg in greeting. Molly froze to the spot. She tried to yell and couldn't. Eventually she made a sound, and then a louder sound and finally screamed for Brendan. He came running, in a panic, expecting to find her bailed up by a crazed Doris, or at the very least a large brown snake.

'What? What is it?' Then, relieved she was okay, he laughed. 'No dunny paper?'

Speechless with fear, Molly pointed to the spider. Brendan followed the line of her trembling finger.

'*That*? Moll, it's just a huntsman.'

She hissed at him, 'Get rid of it!'

Brendan wisely decided not to laugh again. He shrugged instead and, being tall, reached up and plucked the huntsman gently off the splintery lintel and moved it on to a nearby stump.

Molly decamped as fast as she decently could and fled back to the house where Brendan joined her. She was near to tears so he did not joke.

'I'm sorry. I know I'm utterly pathetic and they won't

hurt me and I have to get used to them but it's just they way they look …they're so *hairy*.'

'In their little fur coats,' said Brendan, giving her a hug and failing to mention that the ungrateful wretch had actually bitten him – not badly, but all the same! It wasn't much thanks when he could have so easily got a stick and sent it off to spider heaven. But Molly was off now. Dunny replacement was clearly becoming the number one priority. It was alright for Brendan, who could go behind a tree, but Molly had to sit out there, with spiders and God knows what, while the whole thing threatened to collapse with her inside. Probably in the dark during a thunderstorm. She wanted an inside loo that flushed, was it so much to ask? And Brendan had to agree that it probably wasn't, though they might have to ask Caroline for a loan, which she, being the bookkeeper, would realise. That put a very different complexion on the matter. Molly added insect repellent to her shopping list and vowed to dream up some money-making schemes.

Over breakfast they discussed the day ahead, hoping it would be a little less traumatic than the one just passed. Molly felt she had the better of it, stuck on the farm with a bad-tempered pig, rather than having to deal with the aftermath of the tragedy. Brendan hoped, since he didn't know the people involved personally, that he might be able to ease the load a little for Matron Kurtesz. Molly asked, a little too casually, what this matron was like. Brendan replied, a little too casually, that she was very European.

'Meaning?'

'Oh, you know …'

'No, I don't know.'

'Slim, blonde, elegant. Intriguing accent. Hungarian, I think.'

'Perhaps I should drive you to work,' said Molly. 'I

might need the car.'

Brendan waved the keys at her. 'No you won't. And stop worrying, I think she's a bit sweet on Dr Elliott. Just a feeling.'

At the Secombe farm, breakfast began in silence, the air thick with a quiet desperation. Jenny kept glancing at the phone, hoping Tony would ring and quite unreasonably blaming her father for the fact that he didn't. Hal wondered if he dared speak and was angry that he felt that way in his own house, angry that the loving relationship he'd enjoyed with his daughter had become so fraught that he had to walk on eggshells.

Finally he said, 'This can't go on, Jenny.'

'I don't know what you mean.'

'I think you do. We have to live together in this house. I expect you to behave like an adult. Since you want me to treat you like one.'

'Alright. I'm sorry for what I said last night.'

'It would be nice if you apologised to Vicky.'

'She didn't seem too upset.'

Hal pushed his plate away. He thought wryly that dealing with a problem teenager was a great appetite suppressant, at least he might lose a bit of weight with all that was going on. 'Look,' he said. 'About Vicky and me –'

'Oh, please, no! I don't want to hear! It's none of my business what you do, with Vicky or anyone else. And from now on, it's none of your business what *I* do! Okay?'

Hal took a deep breath. It was getting to be a habit. He said that no, it wasn't okay. She was, after all, only fifteen. She could do what she liked when she truly was an adult. In the meantime, he really didn't know what else she expected of him. He'd written the letter for Dr. Bowen. One of the hardest things he'd ever had to do but he'd done it, it was there on the mantelpiece. What else did she want?

Jenny got up from the table. She told him there was nothing else. Nothing at all. He asked where she was going.

'I thought you wanted me to apologise to Vicky?'

And she left. But Hal suspected that wherever his daughter went that morning, Vicky Dean's surgery would not be her only port of call, though he had a feeling it might be the only one where she would get a good reception. He wished Tony Pieri were a thousand miles away.

Frank Gilroy arrived at the Dean house just as Vicky was getting into her car. He asked after her mother and Vicky said she was alright, feeling a bit washed out like everyone else.

'She said you wanted her help with something.'

'Yes, I do. But I don't want to upset her.'

'She's pretty tough, Frank. Go on in.'

Shirley may have been tough but she nevertheless found it hard to deal with what came next. Frank gave her Elaine's handbag, which he'd found in Ian Sutton's car, and that was bad enough. He wasn't sure what to do with it himself – such a personal, feminine thing, a handbag. Shirley agreed that it was. She'd take it around and quietly give it to Margie, Andy's sister. She could pass it on or not, when the time was right. Frank was grateful.

'There's something else, Shirl. I found this as well. On the floor of the car.'

He held out the wedding ring. Shirley took it and slowly examined it. Aloud, she read the lettering engraved inside: 'E.M. & A.M.'

'I suppose we could give it to the undertaker to put back on her finger. Or give it to Andy. What's best, do you think?'

'Wedding rings don't fall off, Frank.'

'I know, Shirl. I know … that's why I …'

But Shirley, who had tried to be strong, was crying now, uncontrollably and Frank held her, tentatively at first and then more firmly and she sobbed against his shoulder.

Through her tears Shirley thought back to her last conversation with Elaine. She had the terrible feeling that cycling around China together, or anywhere else, had never been a possibility; that Elaine had already decided to spread her wings and fly. Shirley desperately hoped that wasn't true because while she would have found it easy to understand, it would be much harder – remembering Elaine's two boys – to forgive.

After Frank had gone, Shirley decided that although it was Sunday, she'd go into the clinic and do a few jobs that had been overlooked yesterday. She took Elaine's bag with her but did not open it. Had she done so, its contents would have answered a lot of questions.

Sunday or not, animals still got sick and injured. Simon Bowen found Vicky in her surgery, where she'd been attending to a badly mauled cat. He wondered what might have caused it; she thought possibly a dog but more likely a possum. It was a long deep wound low on the cat's right side and extending to its back leg and required a great many stitches. Simon watched with medical interest and admired Vicky's needlework. She thanked him for the compliment and asked what she could do for him; did he perhaps have another dog that needed washing?

Simon was just a bit hurt. 'I came to see how you were getting on. Well, Shirley especially. After yesterday. I mean, I knew Elaine Mackay a little but she was a close friend of your mum's. I thought, if there was anything I could do …'

'Oh, Simon, I'm sorry. That's nice of you. She's okay, I think. Worried about Andy.'

'Will he cope, do you think?'

'Well people do, don't they? Look at Hal Secombe, his wife died of breast cancer when Jenny was barely a teenager.'

'I don't think I've actually met him.'

'Really nice guy.'

There was something about the way she said it that Simon didn't like much but he sensed it wasn't the right time to ask personal questions, not when he was there to enquire about the bereaved. 'Anyway,' Vicky went on, 'Mum's gone into the clinic.'

'Into *work*?'

'There was some stuff that needed doing, she said, and I think she thought it was a good idea to keep busy. I guess that sometimes sitting under a pyramid just doesn't do it.'

'It would never do it for me. At least I'm pretty sure it wouldn't.'

'Frank Gilroy thinks it's a loveable eccentricity.'

'He's rather keen, isn't he?'

'He cooked her dinner last night, gave her a shoulder to cry on. Which was very sweet of him, since I had to go out.'

'I'm sure he didn't find it any hardship.' He refrained, but only just, from asking where Vicky was.

'I'd promised to go to the club with Hal.'

'I see. You and Hal, then …'

'Good friends.'

'Perhaps you'd come out with me, then, since we're friends.'

'I'm rather busy, Dr. Bowen.'

'But there's a really interesting talk at the Historical Society; *Extinction of Local Megafauna –*'

Vicky finished it for him '– *During the Pleistocene*. Sorry, I heard it two years ago. Clem Hill's little biennial treat.'

'Oh. Then I'll go and see if your mother needs any assistance. Goodbye, Dr. Dean.'

'Dr. Bowen. Nice of you to call. Really.' She meant it and he went away thinking that maybe, one day, some dim and future day – and told himself not to be ridiculous, she was probably in love with Hal Secombe – and then he nearly fell over Hal's Secombe's daughter as he opened the front door.

'Jenny!'

'Hi, Dr. Bowen. I'm looking for Vicky, she's wasn't at home.'

'Got an injured cat, go right in.'

Jenny gave him a wan smile and went inside.

CHAPTER EIGHTEEN

The cat was sleeping off the anaesthetic in a cage and Vicky was cleaning up when Jenny knocked tentatively on her consulting room door. Vicky saw Jenny standing there and greeted her warmly. She felt sorry for the poor kid; she thought Jenny looked as though she might run away at any minute.

In fact Jenny wasn't at all sure what she was doing there. She had just been to Tony Pieri's house. It had taken all her courage to go and knock on the front door and it was a long time before anyone answered and when they did it was Tony's younger brother Leo. Leo was actually in the year below Jenny at school and usually treated her like a big sister but this morning he'd been strange; not unfriendly exactly but Jenny had got the very strong feeling that he was lying when he said that Tony was out and sorry, he didn't know where or when he'd be back. He'd almost shut the door in her face. And he left her feeling belittled and needing a woman to talk to.

So when Vicky smiled and said, 'Hi, Jenny, what

brings you here?', Jenny burst into tears. Vicky sat her down and got her a glass of water and when she was coherent, Jenny just said she'd come to apologise for last night. She didn't want Vicky to think she was normally that rude, she was just upset about something else but it was still inexcusable and she was sorry.

Wondering if she were rushing in where angels feared to tread, Vicky surmised that Jenny might be having boy trouble and if so it perhaps wasn't easy, not having a mum to talk to. Jenny flared at that.

'I guess Dad told you the whole story.'

'Your dad loves you. He was a bit lost. He needed someone to talk to as well.'

There was an uncomfortable silence. 'I remember being a teenager,' Vicky said at last. 'God it was awful. Most of the time, anyway.'

'Awful? For you?' Jenny found that hard to believe.

'You bet it was. The other girls all seemed so sure of themselves. They'd talk about their boyfriends and what they'd done and of course I believed them and I wanted to do it too. Sex. They talked about nothing else.'

'It's because I love Tony. That's why I want to go on the pill.'

'And he loves you? He hasn't put any pressure on you, you've made the decision together?'

Jenny wasn't going to answer that, she actually thought Vicky had no right to even ask. Quite forgetting that she'd come here for advice.

'Jenny … I don't want to sound like I know it all because clearly I don't. But I just wonder if you truly do want this right now. If you're really sure about Tony. Because it seems to me that waiting till you're sixteen isn't such a big deal. And you know something else? They say that the pill gives women choice. Which is great. So long as we don't hand that choice over to the guys. Let them use it against us. Know what I mean?'

It was a bit too confronting for Jenny, who really wanted to be told that it was all okay and was pretty sure that she'd already lost her opportunity to make a choice anyway. She thanked Vicky and fled. Vicky sighed and went to check on the cat and thought that felines, who were blissfully lacking in morals, probably had a much easier time of it, possums notwithstanding.

Marta had begun her day with a long ride. She had gone along the river but there was no one swimming this morning so she'd continued up into the foothills. She too had concerns about the day ahead, an uneasy feeling that although it surely could not be worse than yesterday, there was a lot of unfinished business waiting. She was also unusually tired and although she wanted to put it down to the pressure they'd all been under, she had was afraid she might be coming down with something, which was annoying. Like a lot of health professionals, Marta never expected to get sick herself.

She arrived at the hospital late since she was due to stay on for the evening shift and found Terence there looking at Ian Sutton's x-rays. He was pleased to see that they'd achieved perfect alignment with both the tibia and fibula.

'But then they were clean breaks,' he said. 'I'm not quite so happy with the Colles' fracture but I think it'll be okay.'

Marta looked at the x-ray and smiled, it seemed more than okay to her. 'You're too much of a perfectionist, Terence.'

He glanced at her for the first time, ready to deny it, and noticed her drawn appearance. 'You look exhausted,' he said, 'Not getting something, are you?'

Marta denied it vehemently. She wanted to talk about more important things, like the Myers baby. That situation, they both agreed, had to be resolved today.

Strangely enough, they seemed to have come up with the same possible solution.

They were congratulating themselves on their cleverness when they were interrupted by Brendan, clutching two suitcases. He explained that Wally from the garage had dropped them off, they were in the back of Ian Sutton's car. Marta thought it would be more appropriate to take them to Ian's room, until Brendan pointed out that one case was tagged with Elaine Mackay's name.

'Oh dear,' Marta said.

Terence suggested the storeroom next to Marta's office as a temporary holding place and Brendan took the cases away. Terence shook his head. 'The way this is starting to look ...' he said. 'Can you imagine the gossip?'

'Perhaps we should try to find out how it was, Terence. That might be different to how it looks. I'll go and see how Mr Sutton's feeling.'

Ian Sutton's left arm was in plaster and so was his left leg. His head was bandaged. He was mildly concussed, a little confused. Marta said his name but he didn't respond. She touched his shoulder gently and he mumbled something incoherent. It could have been 'Elaine'.

'It's Matron Kurtesz, Mr Sutton, I've come to give you something for the pain.'

But he reached out with his good hand, searching, and this time there was no mistake. 'Elaine, is it you?'

Suddenly, Elaine's last words to Marta came back to her: '*People are sometimes driven to choices which others find incomprehensible. We have to accept that.*' At the time she'd thought it was an odd thing to say. Now she knew it was a plea for understanding. Elaine Mackay and Ian Sutton had indeed loved each other.

Marta drew up Ian's injection and wondered how

quickly the unwelcome truth – or various fanciful versions of it – would spread through Wandin Valley.

Shirley Dean was aware of it already. She'd done the bookwork at the clinic with Elaine's bag beside her and while she kept telling herself she ought not to open it she kept wondering also if maybe it mightn't be best if she did. It's not as if she'd never seen inside it before. If they were in the car together, and Elaine happened to be driving, she had a habit of getting Shirley to retrieve sunglasses or mints or whatever. She had never, as some women do, treated her bag as some private holy of holies. So Shirley, desperate to know the truth, eventually did open it and found nothing but the usual comb and keys and notebook and lipstick and a little case with a couple of emergency tampons, and Elaine's familiar blue wallet which Andy had given her for Christmas a year back. Shirley took the wedding ring now burning a hole in *her* pocket and unzipped the inner compartment of Elaine's handbag. She thought she'd pop the ring in there for safe keeping and give the whole lot back to Andy or his sister later. But there was an envelope in the compartment, a letter in fact. She took it out and looked at it for a long time. The address read:

Andy Mackay
24 Holt Street,
Wandin Valley.

It was in Elaine's handwriting.

Shirley changed her mind about the wedding ring. She finally slipped it into a box of paper clips in her desk drawer.

When Vicky eventually called in a good while later to see if her mum was alright, she found Shirley sitting over a cold cup of tea.

'Are you okay?'

Shirley just shook her head.

'Why don't you go home, Mum? Whatever you're doing here, it can wait.'

'I'm not doing anything. Just worrying about Andy.'

'He'll be okay.'

'No he won't, darling. He won't be okay at all. I've got Elaine's wedding ring in my drawer. Frank found it in Ian's car.'

'Wedding rings don't fall off.'

'No.'

Vicky slumped. 'Actually, it's started already. The gossip. I didn't want to say anything but it was Dot Eskine's cat that got attacked this morning. And I bet she's just the first to ask the question …'

'What was Elaine doing in Ian Sutton's car?'

Vicky nodded. 'How do we keep a lid on it, Mum?'

'By knowing nothing?' But they both knew it would take a miracle. This was a small country town, after all.

Molly Jones thought several times during that Sunday of the tragedy that had engulfed the town; she felt involved because Brendan was involved and she felt especially sorry for those two young boys, on their way home from boarding school to grieve with their father. But she was perhaps the only person in the entire district who was completely, blissfully unaware of the scandal that was perilously close to ruining the lives of several of her new neighbours. Just as well, really. Molly would have told them all to shut up and mind their own business. As it was, she'd spent the morning on a collision course with Doris and had not, regrettably, come out on top.

It had started with the special brunch which Molly had lovingly prepared for the ungrateful swine; it was brunch rather than breakfast because it had taken so long to measure and mix, a gourmet concoction of wheat, bran, milk powder, fish meal and oats. She had carried a large bucket of this to Doris's sty in joyful anticipation of some warm bonding at last.

'Hey, Doris!' Molly had called. 'Wait till you get your fat sides around this!'

But Doris didn't even stir. Molly opened the gate and entered the pen and then, of course, Doris was on her dainty little feet in a flash. She charged Molly, who dropped the bucket, sending the gastronomic wonder in a wild arc all over the sty. Molly made a bolt for the gate and got there just in time, slamming it behind her as Doris propped on the other side. Molly let fly with a stream of invective which would have made Caroline blanch. She was about to march away when she turned back to Doris with a final warming.

'Remember this, you tub of lard. Today's pig can be tomorrow's bacon, got it?'

She went back to the house without her bucket. She was shaking with rage. And, for the second time that morning, she was also very close to tears. She was beginning to see that country life was most definitely not going to be one long romp in a sun-filled paddock of hay. Being Molly Jones, however, she was determined that a spider and a pig were not going to ruin her day. Not entirely.

Someone was also crying at the hospital, a very small someone who remained nameless but whom all the staff had fallen in love with. Judy Loveday had the weekend off but Brendan had snuck into the nursery to try to comfort Miss Myers. Watching him from the door, Marta thought he looked like an old hand.

'You don't have children, do you, Brendan?'

'Not yet, Matron. Planning to, though. I think Molly wants half a dozen. What are you going to do about this little one?'

'I've talked it over with Terence. Something radical, I

think. A last ditch attempt to bring Sandra Myers to her senses.'

'Let's hope it does the trick, then.' Brendan thought he could probably guess what they had in mind; he'd seen it work before and there was no reason to think it wouldn't this time. It was most definitely worth a try.

Back in her office, Marta found Frank Gilroy waiting – more of the unfinished business she'd anticipated. Never one to beat around the bush, he told her she looked terrible. 'Flu, by the look of you, Matron. Why is it that medical people will never give in and admit they're sick?'

'Perhaps, Sergeant Gilroy, because hospitals are like police stations. Understaffed with no-one to fill in for us.'

Frank had to admit she had a point there. He'd come to see if the results of Peter Gleeson's blood tests were back yet and was disappointed to find they weren't. Marta explained that Burrigan pathology was also understaffed, especially at weekends, the results should be back tomorrow. Frank apologised for his edginess.

'It's just that the blood's really all I've got on young Gleeson,' he said. 'Since there wasn't a witness.'

When Frank learned that Peter would be discharged later that day he decided to pay the boy another visit – to read the riot act one more time, as he put it – and stomped off before Marta could intervene. Brendan, who'd overheard some of the conversation, wondered if they need have any fears for the patient's safety.

Peter Gleeson certainly wondered for a minute when the sergeant entered his room, pulled up a chair and sat by his bed once more. But it wasn't anger that emanated from Frank Gilroy but rather an Arctic chill that was even more frightening. The trouble was that Frank could find good in most people, even in a lot of hardened criminals, or he could at least see why they were as they were and make allowances, but he couldn't do that for the likes of Peter Gleeson, who as far as he could see had no excuses, none at all, for throwing his life away.

It was not therefore a long conversation but it was very much to the point. And that was that Peter's long career of drinking and driving and speeding was about to come to an end. He had killed a woman and he would, if there was any justice, be going to jail. He would lose his licence. He had no one to blame but himself, he'd been warned a thousand times about his reckless behaviour and had failed to take any notice whatsoever. Frank was not interested in denials and excuses, the outcome had been both tragic and inevitable. Frank suggested that Peter, when he was discharged, should remember that Elaine Mackay was very much loved in this town and go home the back way. Frank left then and Peter lay there and closed his eyes and buried his face in the pillow. He was still in denial, he still felt badly done by, but perhaps the enormity of what he'd done was beginning to sink in.

CHAPTER NINETEEN

Simon Bowen, who thought he really must take up parachuting or get a hobby like bird-watching because weekends in a country town if you were rostered off were just one enormous drag, had decided to go to the newsagent's to see if he could find something to read. He ended up with *Time* magazine and a murder mystery he was pretty sure he'd read before but he did run into Tim Bourke who'd just finished his paper round. And out of the blue, Simon had an idea.

'Tim,' he said, 'I know I'm getting to be a real bore, but about these headaches – have you got a few minutes?' In the end they went to the milkbar for a very bad coffee and Simon shared his hypothesis. It being Sunday, perhaps if they made a note of everything Tim did, and especially everything he ate and drank, it might give them a clue as to the cause of tomorrow's inevitable migraine. Tim could see the sense in that so they started with the cereal he'd eaten for breakfast, and the lamb roast which would be served for lunch – and which they also had for sandwiches during the week. Dessert varied and no, he hardly ever ate chocolate, he wasn't a big fan. In the afternoon the family would visit or maybe go for a swim and at night they'd go to Lim's. After that, TV and bed.

'Lim's,' said Simon. 'Chinese café, right?' Tim nodded. 'And you go there every week?'

Tim agreed that indeed they did, it saved his mum having to cook and they all enjoyed the food. Well, he and his dad did.

'And when your dad was in the States – did you go to Lim's then?'

Tim couldn't remember at first but Simon hassled him. 'Actually, no,' he said. 'We had fish and chips. Mum reckoned it made a change.'

Simon smiled. 'Do me a favour. Don't eat any Chinese tonight?'

Tim was horrified. 'None at all?'

'Not so much as a dim sim. Just this once, okay? And let me know how you are tomorrow?'

Tim sighed. 'Alright. Anything for medical science.'

Simon left him there, dreaming of prawn toasts, and went off to look in the window of the real estate agent. But while he was checking out the rental listings – and there was one house in Bligh Street that could be a possibility, depending on how much they wanted – something else caught his eye, a reflection from the other side of the street. Tony Pieri's empty panel van was parked outside the garage. Simon saw Jenny Secombe get off her bike and go inside. After a couple of minutes, both Tony and Jenny came out. Jenny looked upset and Simon, feeling for her, thought his real estate business could wait. As though he was unaware of them, he ambled off up the street, glancing at his magazine as he walked.

Jenny had been looking for Tony ever since she'd left Vicky's surgery, determined to find out once and for all where she stood. She could not bear the uncertainty any longer; besides, he owed her five minutes of his time, didn't he? So when she saw his car outside the garage, where Wally Pope let the boys tinker with their vehicles on a Sunday if they behaved themselves, she plucked up all her courage and went in. It had taken some doing, after the reception she'd got at the house, but she'd held her head up and asked, nicely but very firmly, if Tony could spare five minutes and since Wally was there he'd said sure and followed her out. But he wasn't pleased.

'What do you want?'

'To talk.'

'Okay.'

'Not here.'

'Why not here?'

'Tony! It's private.'

Tony looked up and down the near-empty street. Teenage boys can be brutal when they want to be. 'I don't see too many people listening in.'

'Why are you being like this?'

'You know what, Jenny? I don't think there's much to talk about. You go on about how you love me but you aren't too willing to show it, are you?'

'I've explained –'

'Oh, sure. You want me to wait a month. And what then? Another month? Well I'm sick of it. It's not like there's a shortage of girls round here. So I've been asking myself, what am I wasting my time with you for?'

She couldn't believe what she was hearing, the hurt and anger were rising in her like bile. She didn't want to plead with him but she couldn't help it, so much time, so many dreams she had invested here.

'Please, Tony. You don't mean that.'

'Go home to Daddy, Jen. Keep yourself nice for your old age. We're through.' He turned and walked back into the garage without a backward glance.

Jenny heard laughter from his mates inside, awkward, forced laughter. She wished she had the courage to follow Tony in there, to tell him loud and clear how pathetic his behaviour really was, but it was more than she could manage right now. Somehow she got on her bike and rode away.

It was that sort of day in Wandin Valley: challenging. Those who believed in astrology might have gone to check their star charts, the better to prepare themselves for life's little vicissitudes. Marta had rung Bernard Myers earlier that morning and they'd had a little chat; he'd agreed to stay away from the hospital until she gave him the word to come. Now his wife was about to be surprised.

Marta came into Sandra's room wheeling a bassinet. In it was the baby. Sandra sat up, speechless at first and shook her head. Marta positioned the bassinet alongside her bed. 'It's time you got to know each other.'

'I don't want her here.'

'But she wants to be with you, Mrs. Myers. And quite frankly, we need you to look after her. We've had a tragic weekend here. We've all lost a dear friend. The man in the room to your right has multiple injuries. Everyone is in shock. You, however, are blessed with a beautiful little girl. New life, new hope. I leave her with you.'

Marta left. She didn't dare look back but Brendan passed by the open door soon after and saw that Sandra had turned her back on the baby and was staring fixedly at the wall.

'Wait till she cries,' he said to Marta and Terence in the office.

'I'm the one who'll be crying if it doesn't work,' said Marta.

'Time,' said Terence. 'Give it time.' But the baby, who had been well fed and was generally a contented little thing, had done her crying much earlier in the day and now slept peacefully through what remained of the morning, through lunchtime, when Sandra refused to eat, and through the early afternoon, leaving her distraught father to fret the hours away in a dreary motel room.

Molly, meanwhile, had decided that the question of Doris was another which required an immediate solution. The pig had challenged her authority and must be taught that such behaviour wasn't acceptable. Molly, however, had no idea about how to train a pig. She rather doubted in any case that a pig of Doris's age could be persuaded to change her ways. She was searching through her books on pig-raising for enlightenment when Vicky Dean made a very welcome appearance at her door. Vicky had come to see how Molly was getting on. Molly gave it to her straight.

'Honestly, if I hadn't let Brendan take the car this morning, I would have been bashing on your door. That rotten pig tried to kill me.'

'Shall we have a cup of tea? I brought some scones and jam, gift of another grateful client.'

Molly put the kettle on and felt a little abashed. 'I'm a grateful client too. I just haven't had time for baking. You must think I'm hopeless.'

'No, I don't. I think Doris probably needs mating.'

'Really? Well she made me feel incompetent. I mean – she charged me. Knocked the bucket right out of my hand. And I really hate to admit this … I was scared.'

'That's an awful lot of pig, Molly.'

Molly sighed. 'What do I do now?'

'You could give Doris the chop and buy a couple of slips.'

'Um – slips?'

'Sorry. Piglets, straight off the mother. You'd all get used to each other while you fattened them up.'

Molly thought about it while she made the tea and decided it wasn't such a good idea. Cute little piglets would end up as pets, she'd worry about them on cold nights. Vicky laughed and wondered if Molly was quite sure that farming was for her. Molly smiled.

'You know I told you I worked in the fashion industry?' Vicky nodded. 'Can you imagine what that was like? It's got nothing to do with reality. It's a fantasy world. People with too much money who think that dressing up will make them feel younger and happier and better than everyone else. It doesn't, of course, so they come back next week to try again. I'd had enough of sucking up to that lot. I think I'd rather try my luck with Doris.' Vicky grinned and smeared thick strawberry jam on a scone and passed it to her. 'Ta. And you don't get scones and jam like this in the city.'

'I'd still sell Doris.'

'I will not be beaten by a pig.'

'Okay. Then you'll need to toughen up as far as animals are concerned. I should take you out to the abattoir.'

'I'm game. I think we should all know where our food comes from.'

Vicky was surprised at her enthusiasm. 'And if you like, you could spend some time at the surgery. You'd learn a bit there.'

'Sounds good. Oh, look, I'm a whiz with a sewing machine. Maybe I could make you something. Just to say thanks for your help?'

Vicky couldn't help glancing at Molly's outfit. How to decline as gracefully as possible? But Molly burst out laughing. 'Oh, no, not the sort of gear that *I* wear. It's hardly you, is it? I meant something nice and well – country.'

Vicky was relieved. 'That'd be great. Thank you.'

Molly asked her then about the accident. 'I should have mentioned it before. Brendan said the lady who died was a friend of your mother's.'

'Yes, she was. They were pretty close.'

'I'm so sorry. You shouldn't be out here worrying about me.'

'Mum's okay. I think she needed a bit of space. I'll stay home with her this evening, let her talk if she wants to. Answer the phone, that's the main thing.'

'I suppose people rally around.'

'Yes, they do. Mum's the rallying type. But others – they gossip. There's been quite a bit of that today. Shall we go and tell this pig what's what?'

Baby Myers was probably getting hungry. Or she had a wet nappy. Or most likely both. Her first tentative cries gradually became louder and louder. Terence stopped trying to persuade Marta that she was too sick to work and they both listened. The sound could easily be heard from the office so in Sandra's room it was very loud indeed.

Sandra buried one ear against the pillow and put a hand over the other. It did no good whatsoever. The cries became a piercing wail, stopped for a second while the baby drew a shuddering breath then restarted with increased energy and volume. It was a primeval howl for attention and no mother, not even Sandra Myers in her present state of mental anguish, could deny it. She slowly reached out a hand and rocked the bassinet. It took some time but the cries began to diminish. She continued to rock. The cries died away. There was a tiny gurgle.

Painfully, Sandra eased herself into a semi-upright position, from where she could look into the bassinet. Two blue eyes looked up into hers. She put a finger into a tiny hand which curled around it.

'Hello,' she whispered. 'Hello, you.'

Brendan had joined Terence and Marta. The three of them listened to the blissful sound of silence. It was quite a while before Sandra's bell rang.

'I'll go,' Marta said.

'And while you're gone, I'm ringing Molly,' Brendan said, 'to tell her I'm covering your night shift. You have to go home.'

'Doctor's orders, Marta. You need aspirin and bed.'

'Alright. I give in. Thank you. I'll go very soon.'

Marta did not want to get too close to the baby but she could see that all was well as soon as she entered Sandra's room.

'There's no mistake? She is mine?'

Marta smiled. 'This is a very small hospital. We don't have a nursery full of babies. What are you going to call her?'

'Bernie's mother's name is Sarah. So I think – Rachel.'

Marta grinned. 'Shall I tell him he can come?'

Sandra shook her head. 'He's seen her?'

'Yes.'

'Then he can wait for a bit. I want some time to get to know her. Tell him he can join us for dinner. If I'm going to forgive him, I'll take my time over it. Can I pick her up?'

'Of course.'

Sandra took the baby out of the bassinet and held her. The baby nuzzled against her and sought her breast. Marta nodded encouragingly.

'Do you think I'm being too hard on him?'

Marta let that go. 'I'm just very glad that Rachel will have two parents.'

'You've all been very patient with me. You and Dr Elliott especially.'

'You had a difficult time.'

'He's good, isn't he, Dr Elliott? Good-looking too. Is he married?'

'Not now.'

'Then what are you waiting for, Matron?'

Marta covered well. 'I'll ring your husband, Mrs. Myers, and then I'm going home, I seem to be getting flu. Look after that beautiful baby.' She left then and did not hear what Sandra whispered to her baby. It was just girl talk but closer to the truth than Sandra could have guessed.

CHAPTER TWENTY

Needless to say Doris had behaved like a perfect lady in Vicky's presence though there were of course no guarantees that it would last. Molly was asking about Bob Hatfield's suggestion of alcohol as a porcine relaxant when the phone rang. It was Brendan explaining Marta's illness and the need for him to work late. Molly tried hard to hide her disquiet, reassuring him that it didn't worry her in the least, she wasn't the slightest bit nervous about being on her own, and if she couldn't keep the generator going, she'd just have to turn Doris into lard and make candles of her – which was about what she deserved. Molly did not altogether convince Brendan but there wasn't a lot he could do about it. She didn't convince Vicky at all.

'Brendan's working late.'

'Yes. The matron's sick. It's nice that she trusts him to take over already.'

'Except that you *are* nervous.'

Molly tried to laugh it off. 'Me? Good heavens no! I'll get on with some sewing, I'll be absolutely fine.'

'Are you sure?'

'Yes!' And then her resolution crumbled a little. 'I just didn't realise, you know, that it would be quite so lonely out here. Just a pig and a spider for company.' She shivered a little. Vicky didn't laugh, she really felt for her.

'I'll be home. If it gets too much, give me a ring. And think about getting a dog. You need someone to talk to while Brendan's working. A pig and a huntsman don't really cut it.' Which at least made Molly smile again.

Marta was still at the hospital, still finding things that she needed to check on, things that only she could do. She'd already given Bernard Myers the message from his wife and he'd been almost pathetically grateful for all that she and Terence had done to promote his cause. Marta gave credit to the baby. She said everyone made mistakes and it was now up to Sandra and Bernard to see if they could put the past behind them; she very much hoped that they could.

Brendan was more concerned about Ian Sutton who still didn't know that Elaine Mackay was dead. He was relieved when Marta told him Terence would come back to see Ian later. He would probably break the news then.

'If he loved her,' Brendan said, 'then God help him.'

'His loss is no greater than Andy Mackay's, Brendan.'

'I was talking about the dilemma he'll be facing, Matron.'

'Oh. I see. Indeed.' Marta was struck again by his sensitivity. She pressed a hand to her throbbing temple.

'Ian did love Elaine Mackay, didn't he?' Marta just nodded, suddenly just too weary to think about it any more. 'Go home, Matron. I can always ring you if the skies fall in.'

So Marta went home without telling Brendan or anyone else that she had opened the two suitcases in the storeroom and gone through their contents. One had clearly contained Ian's clothes so presented no problem, it could go home with him. But the other case contained a woman's clothes and Marta actually recognised some of them. They had belonged to Elaine Mackay and with them was a framed photo of her boys so improbable scenarios involving the loan of the case and clothes for the op shop made no sense. Marta had thought hard about what to do with the case and had decided to hang on to it, at least for now. She could not see what would be achieved by handing it over either to Andy or to Frank Gilroy. And if that meant she was committing some sort of misdemeanour (she did not for a minute regard it as a crime) then so be it.

For an hour or two after she left Tony Pieri, Jenny Secombe just kept riding. Jenny was a country girl at heart but at times like this she longed for the anonymity of a big city; unless she rode deep into the bush somewhere, which wasn't that easy on a bike like hers, there was nowhere to really escape in Wandin Valley; no coffee shop where she could sit unnoticed, no mall where she could pretend to shop for hours; there were simply no public spaces where she wouldn't be seen and recognised. She did go to Louise's place but Louise and her mum were off in Magnolia Vale for the day. She even considered calling in on her Aunt Helen; not that she got on with her Aunt Helen all that well, Aunt Helen was a bit too churchy for Jenny, her relationship with Jesus so personal that it made Jenny a little uncomfortable to hear her talk about it. All the same, she loved Jenny like a daughter and Jenny was in need of all the affection she could get right now. But she decided against it. Aunt Helen had never approved of Tony Pieri and would doubtless see the hand of her Almighty Friend in the demise of the relationship.

So finally Jenny did what she should have done in the first place and went home. Hal knew something was wrong the minute she got off her bike. He was still milking but she looked over towards him and waved and he waved back as they always did but the way she turned and tramped off towards the house, head down, it all spelled out despair. The milking had to be finished. Hal thought that, anyway, it was probably best to give her time, she mightn't want to talk about it, she might just want to lie on her bed and have a good cry.

Which is what Jenny did, and by the time her father finally came in she was a bit red-eyed still but otherwise more or less composed and boiling some eggs to go in a salad, since it was still pretty hot.

'I thought we'd just have something cold, is that okay?'

'Good idea,' Hal said. 'You wonder when the change is ever going to come. You need any help?' Jenny shook her head. Her father felt helpless. He desperately wanted to tell her it would be all right, that the hurt she was feeling would not go on forever. He also wanted to go and find Tony Pieri, whom he was pretty damn sure had caused the hurt, and break his neck. 'I might just have a quick shower then,' he said.

It wasn't until the evening meal – the salad and eggs and tomatoes and cold corned beef – was nearly over that Jenny finally said, 'I saw Vicky Dean today.'

Hal was non-committal. 'Oh yes.'

'She's nice. No – she's smart. I mean – both. She said something that really hit home. We were talking about the pill and she said how it's supposed to give women choice. But we had to be careful that we didn't hand that choice over to the guys. We had to make sure they didn't use it to put pressure on us.' She paused and then she looked at Hal. 'That's what Tony did. It's *exactly* what Tony did.' Her voice, which had been strong, fell to a whisper. 'I feel such a fool, Dad.'

Hal knew it was over then but of course he didn't rejoice, he loved her far too much for that. He got up and went to her and hugged her and told her that she deserved so much more than Tony Pieri, he was the fool and all she had to do was hold her head high because she had nothing at all, nothing, to reproach herself for. And deep down she knew that while it might take a while before the pain went away, her father on this occasion was right.

They talked about growing up for a while and how a new approach might be required, with more listening and less shouting on both sides and Jenny thought that if her dad wanted to take Vicky Dean out it would be okay with her. She seemed quite disappointed when Hal informed her they were just good friends.

It was a very tentative Bernard Myers who arrived at his wife's hospital room that evening. He was usually the most confident of men, he'd even been called brash on occasion; the sort of man who let his passion and enthusiasm run away with him. Which is what had got him into trouble at the awards night. Right now he wasn't at all sure what to expect. He wasn't even sure how to behave. He just knew that he loved his wife and he'd do anything on God's earth to get her back.

'Sandy?' he said from the doorway, not just tentative but positively timid.

The baby was now sound asleep in the bassinet. Sandra put a finger to her lips and beckoned him in. He stood by the bed and looked down at them both.

'She's beautiful, isn't she? I've called her Rachel.'

'Rachel. That's a lovely name. Rachel Sandra would be nice.'

'Rachel Sarah.' Sandra held out her arms to him then and he kissed her and hugged her and begged her forgiveness and vowed it would never happen again and she said he'd be too busy with two women at home to look after to go chasing after any others.

'I tried to bring you flowers,' he said. 'But it's Sunday, the dry cleaners were shut.'

'The dry cleaners?' It only took Sandra a moment. 'Oh! Country towns.' She laughed. 'I don't need flowers.'

Terence heard the laughter as he passed and was relieved. One small success. He knew that the visit he was about to make would have no such happy outcome. He went into Ian Sutton's room and Brendan reported on the patient's condition and left him to the grim task ahead.

'How are you feeling, Ian?'

'Not too bad, doc. Bit of pain, still.'

'The damage you've suffered, I'm afraid it has to be expected. But if it gets too much, just let the nursing staff know. Don't be a martyr, we don't believe in agony.'

'It's bearable.'

'Good.'

'Do you remember what happened, Ian?' Here I am, about to inflict the agony, Terence thought.

'Hardly remember a thing. They've had me on so much dope. The nurse – Brendan, is it? – said a two-car collision?'

'That's right. At Five Mile Creek.'

Ian just shook his head. 'I wasn't driving fast, in fact Elaine kept saying we'd never –' He broke off suddenly. 'No-one's mentioned Elaine, is she alright?'

Terence took a deep breath. He told himself there was no point in delaying this. Suddenly Ian started to panic.

'She's alright, isn't she? Please tell me – she is alright?'

'I'm sorry, Ian. Mrs. Mackay's dead. She was brought back here and we operated but … she never regained consciousness.'

Ian just shook his head, back and forth, in total disbelief. Terence saw that he was crying though no sound came. There was silence for a long time. At last Ian said, a statement of fact, 'I killed her.'

'No. It wasn't your fault.'

'All the same …'

'It was not your fault, Ian. The other driver was to blame.'

'We thought we were starting a new life. She was like a girl, excited … she can't be dead! Oh, Elaine …!' It was a cry of pure anguish.

Terence passed Marta's house on his way home and saw that her living-room light was on. He needed someone to talk to and thought if she were really ill, he wouldn't stay but he could always make her a hot lemon drink. She was actually glad to see him. She'd managed a few hours sleep earlier and said she was sure she had felt worse, though she wasn't sure when. She apologised for her appearance – she was in a dressing-gown – and Terence said she looked fine (he thought she looked a great deal more than fine, in fact) and made tea for them both. And then they talked. Terence had found his discussion with Ian discomforting; the fact that Ian had never once mentioned Andy Mackay, who was supposed to be his friend and who had lost his wife.

Marta then told Terence about the contents of the suitcases and what she had decided to do. 'So Andy Mackay lost his wife before the accident, Terence. He just didn't know it.' Marta said.

'Then somehow we have to make sure that he never finds out.'

'Is that possible, do you think?'

'I don't know, Marta. We have to try. Or Andy will be destroyed.'

But as Vicky had predicted early in the day, the Wandin Valley rumour mill had not taken long to crank into action and it was doubtful now if anyone could put a brake on it. That at least, was Frank Gilroy's opinion. He'd called to see Andy and found him in a bad way. Margie, his sister, was clearly concerned. The two boys sat on the couch, staring blindly at the television, red-eyed, lost, and the phone rang constantly. Andy refused to answer it or to talk to people. He didn't like what they were saying, what they were implying. He kept asking Frank for details of the accident, exactly what Frank had found when he got there. Given Andy's mental state, Frank was reluctant to discuss it. He said there'd be plenty of time for that. Tomorrow he was expecting to lay charges, then it would all be up to the court, the truth would come out, speculation wouldn't help anyone. He took Andy outside, tried to suggest that it wasn't good for the boys to hear all this talk and Andy eventually calmed down a little and agreed that no, it wasn't.

He seemed quieter after Frank had gone and briefly sat with Chris and Joel and talked about flowers for the funeral. Elaine loved yellow roses so they settled on those. Then Joel, the younger boy, who had never been to a funeral, wanted to know what would happen and if the man who killed their mum would be there. It was more than Andy could cope with. He looked pleadingly at Margie and fled the scene to take himself on a long walk through the quiet evening streets of Wandin Valley, hoping to sort out the turmoil in his mind.

CHAPTER TWENTY-ONE

Molly Jones was dealing with turmoil of a different kind. Doris was not the problem this evening, that is, she wasn't a problem any more. After she'd played her usual trick of kick the bucket when Molly presented her evening meal, and done a little pretend charge to show who was boss, Molly had resorted to the Bob Hatfield remedy. Brendan had a six pack of beer in the fridge and Molly fed first three and then another three bottles to Doris. After that she became surprisingly amenable. Molly decided she would need to do a short course in home brewing and put it on her list.

But with Doris virtually non compos another problem remained and that was the generator. It had positively purred along for most of the day, apart from one or two little hiccups to which Molly had applied some judicious cranking. But then, in those moments when twilight began to fade, just as Molly was threading up her sewing machine, there was a rather larger hiccup. The light in the kitchen flickered. She looked up at it balefully. It brightened, went out, came back on, tormenting her. It stayed bright until darkness fell, during which time Molly lined up a torch. And then it began to dim again.

'It's in league with Doris,' she said aloud. And as if in agreement, the light went out and stayed out. Molly grabbed the torch. She shone it outside. Blackness. The moon was not yet up. She pulled the curtain across, she felt strangely exposed. She took a deep breath and went outside to the shed where the generator lay sulking. She talked to it. Nicely at first and then forcefully and cranked with all her might and main but the generator did not respond. With some distaste she brushed the cobwebs from the hurricane lamp hanging on the wall nearby and took it inside where she eventually got it alight. But she could not sew because her machine required power. As did the television. The radio had a battery but tonight – she had seen it in the guide – they were playing excerpts from *The Ring Cycle.* Long, long, excerpts. Molly sighed and picked up *Pig Farming For Fun and Profit.*

Simon had been right about the murder mystery, he had read it before. A third of the way in, the resolution came back to him in fine detail and he chucked it aside and opted for a vaguely interesting wildlife documentary on the ABC. Vast herds of wildebeest were migrating across the Serengeti when Andy Mackay knocked on his door. Simon was surprised that Andy even knew where he lived but invited him in. Andy apologised profusely for interrupting Simon at home; he should have waited till morning, gone to see Simon at the surgery – Simon interrupted him.

'Mr. Mackay, please. You're not interrupting anything. Believe me, there's only so many times a man can watch the great migration of the wildebeest. Come and sit down.'

Andy sat. Simon thought he looked terrible, which

was hardly surprising. 'What can I do for you, Mr Mackay? I'm sure you haven't had much sleep, I could give you something.'

'Andy, please. You knew Elaine, didn't you?'

'Just a little. She was often in the surgery, seeing Shirley Gilroy about this and that.'

'She said you were a breath of fresh air.' For some reason that simple remark pleased Simon enormously.

'You know how much we all admired her, Andy. The work she did.'

Andy nodded, accepting this. 'There are just some questions, doctor. I tried to ask Frank Gilroy but the boys are home ... it was difficult. Frank said it would all come out eventually. And yes, no doubt it will. But there are things I need to know now. You were there at the accident. Maybe you can tell me.'

'I didn't see it happen –'

'No, I understand. But you stopped to help, right?' Simon nodded. 'Could you tell me exactly what you found?'

Simon was a bit thrown by that request but he thought he could guess what prompted it. Even in the newsagent's, he'd picked up on the gossip. Andy must know, or suspect, what people were saying and he wanted the truth. Or thought he did, which was another thing altogether. Simon chose his words carefully.

'I'm a doctor, Andy, not a policeman. My first thought – my only thought – was could I help? I just registered that two vehicles were involved. One was only lightly damaged, with the driver sitting outside of it. The other had hit a tree and the occupants were still inside so I rushed to that car first.'

'Ian Sutton's station wagon.'

Simon nodded. 'It had his business name on the side. I'd never met Ian. He was the driver. Your wife was in the passenger seat. They were both unconscious. I did a medical assessment as quickly as I could while Frank was calling the ambulance. Elaine was in a bad way, worse off than Ian, bleeding internally. But she didn't suffer, she wouldn't have felt any pain. I am absolutely sure of that.'

'Which way was it pointing?'

'The car?'

'Yes. I mean, what direction was it travelling?'

'Well, when I got there, south I suppose. Yes, south. But the impact could have caused it to spin around, it's impossible to say where it was going originally.'

'And you didn't talk to Ian?'

'No, like I said, he was unconscious too. He's a friend of yours, yes?'

'That's right. Known him most of my life.'

'He's doing alright. He'll make a full recovery. I mean, as much as one ever does recover from something like this.'

But Andy wasn't thinking about Ian. 'If the car was heading south – well that doesn't make sense. That's heading to Melbourne.'

Simon tried to make light of it. 'Awful lot of places before Melbourne. Maybe they were going to one of the vineyards.'

'Something like that. Elaine just got a lift somewhere.'

Simon thought, he's trying to convince himself and it's not really working. Andy got up and Simon quickly went to his medical bag. 'Andy, it's a terrible time. There's so much to think about and you've got those boys depending on you to stay strong. I'm going to give you a mild sedative, just to help you get some sleep. There's a prescription you can get made up tomorrow … and here's a couple for tonight, okay?'

'I'm sure I can manage.'

'You're not Superman. You'll manage better with a

little help.' Andy saw the sense in that, or pretended to, and took the prescription from Simon. Simon walked out with him and when he saw that Andy was on foot, offered to drive him home but Andy insisted the walk would help to clear his head and disappeared into the night. But he did not go home.

Simon wasn't the only one concerned about Andy Mackay. Frank Gilroy had seen enough during his years in the force to know that everyone dealt with grief in their own way but Andy wasn't just grieving. Frank felt he was watching Andy fumble for the key to a dark room that was filled with unnamed horrors; he was afraid that Andy would unlock the door and go inside. He did not mean to say any of this to Shirley Dean when he called to make sure she was alright. Vicky answered the door and he was glad to see her.

'Oh Vicky, you're home. Good. I heard about the Thompson's mare and I thought maybe you'd get called out.'

'No, thank goodness. Not laminitis after all, it seems to have improved a bit. Come in.'

'No, look, I just thought I'd check that Shirl was okay, but since you're here …'

But Shirley had heard his voice and called him herself. 'Frank, thank God, you gave me an excuse to get off the phone. Sit down, have a drink.' She held out her glass to Vicky who obediently refilled it. Frank shook his head. 'Damn Esme Watson. The gall of the woman. How the hell should I know what Elaine was doing in Ian Sutton's car? And why should I or anyone care? These people!' Her anger was very quickly turning to tears but both Frank and Vicky ignored them. 'Maybe Elaine's car played up at the last minute. Or Ian asked her to help with something … or … what does it *matter*? But clearly it does because the phone hasn't stopped. I hope to heaven they're not ringing Andy.' Frank didn't respond. 'My God, they are.'

'I'm afraid so.'

Shirley found the tissues. Vicky offered Frank a glass of wine again and since he was off duty, this time he accepted. Shirley thought she might hang on to Elaine's bag until after the funeral and Frank thought that was a good idea.

'And the wedding ring,' Shirley said. 'I think, like you said – if I gave it to the Funeral Directors – let them just slip it on her finger? Then no one would be any the wiser.'

And Frank said gently that he'd thought about it too and yes, that seemed the best idea. He drank the wine and left soon after, having reassured himself that everything was under control in the Dean household. Vicky thought, not for the first time, what a decent bloke he was. Maybe Shirley thought much the same thing, however reluctantly.

Feminist though she was, Molly had to admit that she could do with the help of a bloke on this particular night when her own was engaged elsewhere. The trouble began with the patter of tiny feet in the roof. Molly tried to tell herself it was sweet little furry possums she could hear but she knew damn well it was really the less favoured species of *rattus Rattus*, or possibly, this far inland, *rattus Norvegicus*. Aside from unwelcome visitors, the hurricane lamp was rapidly running out of kero. Molly knew there must be more but she did not know where. She did not fancy searching the barn and the shed, both festooned with cobwebs, by the light of a small torch. Nor did she want to ring Brendan who, she was sure, had quite enough on his plate without being troubled by a sooky wife.

She tried to conjure the generator back into life, first

with sweet-talking, then by cranking and finally with what she felt was a rather vicious kick. The generator failed to respond. She was left with the option of reading by torchlight or copping out and ringing the Wandin Valley Pump Company. She rang. Bob Hatfield, who was far too much of a gentleman to say 'I told you so', arrived twenty minutes later.

Bob was more than a technician. He was an engineer. An artist, even. He not only knew to kick the generator, but where and how hard. The problem, he explained to Molly, was her choice of footwear. Fluffy purple ugg boots were simply never going to deliver sufficient force. He recommended that she invest in a pair of Blunnies or Redbacks or something like that. Something with a bit of heft. Molly nodded and tried to look knowledgeable. Bob showed her how to deliver the irresistible blow and the genny burst into joyous life. Molly was so filled with joy herself she hugged him. They had a cup of coffee and for a while after the Wandin Valley Pump Company had departed, the night did not seem so empty nor the darkness outside so – well, black. Molly went back to her sewing, something which always gave her pleasure, and ceased to look at the clock every five minutes. She thought she would get through the night without any problems.

At the hospital, most of the patients had settled down. Bernard Myers had returned to his motel to sleep soundly. His wife was doing the same – or rather, she was making the most of it until baby Rachel awoke and demanded attention.

Ian Sutton, scarcely able to move because of his injuries, slept only when the pethidine allowed it; most of the time he lay there tormented by grief, alone with his loss. He knew where the town's sympathies would lie once the news of the affair got out; it would be all for

Andy Mackay, it would wrap its arms around him like a blanket. Ian himself would be cast into outer darkness and he cared not a whit about that but what of Elaine? Would they rip her down from her pedestal and throw her to the wolves? Well it couldn't hurt her now. Such small minds, they would never, ever understand. They lived in a world of absolutes, of black and white, of right and wrong. They had no doubt seen him and Andy as two of a kind: decent, salt of the earth country blokes, mates you could rely on, pillars of the community. And that is why they would find this whole business so terribly, even deliciously, shocking. But they were wrong, Andy and Ian were nothing alike at all.

It was Ian and Elaine who had gradually realised they were twin spirits, both kicking against the pricks of life in a small country town, desperate to discover something altogether grander on which to expend their energies. They had decided to seek it together, to start all over again. They had spent too many seasons in quiet valleys. It was time to try life at the top of the mountain, across the ocean, amongst the stars.

Love, they thought foolishly, would conquer all. In time they would be forgiven; they would come back to visit; the boys would spend holidays with them in Bali or Perth or Singapore or wherever they happened to be. Andy would move on and if they did not end up friends exactly, at least it would be civilised. They were probably dreaming to think that but people in love are often delusional.

Ian heard the little baby cry in the next room. He did not have children; his ex-wife had not been able to and neither of them had wanted to adopt. It had probably contributed to the divorce in the end but that was many years ago. He accepted that Elaine loved him when he realised she was willing to leave her boys to be with him, to jeopardise her relationship with them for his sake. The enormity of it overwhelmed him.

The hospital had been so quiet. Now he heard sounds. There was the low voice of the woman in the next room, hushing the baby, feeding her no doubt; then a shrill, older voice, the woman who always wanted tea. Dear God, who drank tea at midnight?

Brendan was trying, as gently as he could, to persuade Miss Bird that it was not a good idea. Tea, he said, was a diuretic. If she drank any more she'd be up all night, wanting to go to the toilet. Neither she nor anyone else would get any sleep. How much better to snuggle down and look forward to a wonderful cuppa first thing in the morning.

'I could die in the night,' she said. 'How would you feel then, knowing you'd denied an old woman her last wish? Let me tell you, when I was droving cattle out on the Castlereagh –'

'Birdie,' Brendan said, 'I'm afraid it's time to accept that your droving days are over. You're not looking after two thousand head any more, it's just me looking after you. Happens to all of us. Be a dear, don't make it hard for me.'

'Oh alright, then. Just because I like you, young Brendan.' And to Brendan's relief she did indeed try to snuggle down. He pulled the blanket up and patted her thin old shoulder and tip-toed out, congratulating himself. He did not know that while he was spending rather too much time indulging Miss Bird, Andy Mackay had slipped into the hospital unseen.

CHAPTER TWENTY-TWO

Andy wanted answers to the questions which were tormenting him, ones he was terrified that Chris, his elder son, would soon be asking too; questions which neither Frank Gilroy nor Simon Bowen had been able to answer. Andy thought Ian Sutton was probably the only person who could. After he left Simon's flat he walked, barely knowing where he was headed, all the way to the hospital and there he was, in the middle of the night, going from room to room.

He eventually found Ian and paused by the bed, taken aback by what he could see in the half-light of Ian's injuries. Ian lay on his back, his head turned away, he appeared to be asleep.

'Ian?' There was no response and Andy didn't know where to touch him to evoke one without doing any damage; hard to avoid the drip lines and bandages and plaster. He spoke again, louder, 'Ian? Mate, it's me, Andy. Just need to talk for a bit.'

Fortunately Brendan arrived then and put a firm arm around Andy and led him away. 'Come on, Mr. Mackay this is no time for visiting, is it? You can come back tomorrow and see your friend when everyone's feeling a bit brighter.'

Ian Sutton heard the calming words fade away down the corridor and opened his eyes and stared at the wall and let out a long breath. He knew he would have to face Andy sometime. He just had to find the courage.

Molly had got on with her sewing with no further interruptions and was feeling quite pleased with herself. She had even for a while decided that Wagner had his uses after all, the Valkyries having for a while drowned out the high jinks in the roof. But she could only stand so much of Hitler's favourite musician and had turned it off about the time Siegfried came into possession of Alberich's cursed ring. It was not a wise move. Not long after, just as she was trying to convince herself that it was perfectly safe to go to the loo, that she couldn't possibly come to any harm whatsoever, a strange hooting noise started up outside the partially open window. Molly abruptly sat down again. The eerie sound continued; eerie, that is, to anyone unfamiliar with the tawny frogmouth. Molly was a sensible girl. It might sound like a ghost but it most definitely wasn't. She strode to the door and opened it. 'Is there anybody there?' she said, much like Walter de la Mare's Traveller. The response was a rush of wings, much too close, and then silence. Molly shivered. 'Come home, Brendan,' she whispered. Then, telling herself to get a grip, she tried to go back to her sewing. But the fright and the earlier coffee with Bob Hatfield were having their effect. A visit to the dunny was becoming a matter of urgency. The lights flickered and went out just as the hooting started again. Molly started to laugh, just a little hysterically.

'An owl,' Molly said. 'That's what it is! A nice owl of

some sort who will eat the rats. I am *not* frightened of owls.' She did not expect her resolve to last more than five minutes. She grabbed the torch, found a pair of Brendan's boots and put them on. She went out to the shed and kicked the genny in the guts. It was so surprised it came to life. She went to the dunny. She returned to the house. And that was it. She went to bed and hid under the blankets. She did not sleep at all until Brendan got home in the early hours of the morning.

'How did you manage, all alone out here?'

'Piece of cake,' Molly said.

'So brave.' He hugged her and found she was trembling. He grinned. 'And such a bad liar.'

'I'll get used to it, darling. It might just take a little while.'

'Night shift always does. Want to join me in a beer?'

'It's nearly breakfast time.'

'Not for me, it isn't. For me it's the end of a long working day. Beer time.'

'Um, Brendan. Bit of bad news …'

When Terence arrived at the hospital on the Monday morning he was surprised to find Marta already there. 'You should be in bed,' he said.

'It's just as well I'm not, already I've got two big problems to deal with.' She showed him a note that Brendan had left, about Andy Mackay's nocturnal visit to Ian Sutton. They both found it disturbing, he would doubtless return today and they could hardly stop him visiting a man who was purportedly a close friend. Terence volunteered to speak to Ian Sutton again.

'But possibly even worse than that,' Marta went on, 'I've had a call from the pathology lab in Burrigan. Finally they've got the results on Peter Gleeson's blood sample.' She sighed deeply.

'And?'

'Sergeant Gilroy is going to be furious. But it seems that the sample was contaminated.'

'What? How on earth ...?'

'I don't know, Terence. I don't know how on earth. Frank's on his way. You'd better speak to Ian.'

'That can wait till Frank's been. I might be able to prevent an arrest. Or a homicide.'

Simon Bowen, holding the fort at the surgery, had asked Shirley for Andy Mackay's card and filled in the details of the medication he'd prescribed.

'I'm not asking you to break patient confidentiality, Simon – but was he alright?'

'He wanted information about the accident. I couldn't really help. And no – he wasn't alright. But then, who would be?'

Mrs Bourke arrived then, a gushing and gratified Mrs Bourke, to tell Simon that he was, in short, a miracle worker. Tim had got up this morning, fresh as a daisy, not a hint of a migraine, and gone off to school. 'How did you know it was Chinese food?'

'Not Chinese food, exactly, Mrs. Bourke. MSG. Monosodium glutamate, which is just a flavour enhancer. It's not an allergen but some people – and Tim seems to be one of them – have an intolerance to it. Hence the migraines.'

'Well you've hit the nail on the head. Lim's will have to do without us on Sunday nights, or Tim will have to make do with fish and chips or something. His dad's none too thrilled – I mean, he's pleased for Tim but he does love his sweet and sour prawns. Never mind, a small price to pay and we can't thank you enough.'

'I'm just glad we managed to solve the problem, Mrs. Bourke. I wish they were all that simple in the end.'

He escaped into his surgery, leaving Shirley to deal with Dorothy Bourke. 'I had my doubts about him at first,' Dorothy said. 'But he's come up trumps.'

'Yes,' said Shirley. 'Never pays to rush to judgement, does it?'

'I wouldn't want to do that about Elaine Mackay,' said Dorothy, 'but it does look bad, doesn't it?'

'I heard her car wouldn't start,' Shirley said, 'and Ian gave her a lift. Then someone said they'd gone mushrooming. Someone else insisted they were doing speed trials for a charity car rally. And – quite ridiculous this one – they were actually running away together! Did you ever hear such nonsense!'

To her credit, Dorothy Bourke felt a little ashamed. 'You're right, Shirley. We should all mind our own business. It's a tragedy however it happened.' And she left, leaving Shirley feeling that maybe, just maybe, there would still be a future in Wandin Valley for Andy Mackay.

Frank had arrived at the hospital to get the results of Peter Gleeson's blood sample. He already knew there was a problem and Marta was right, he was very angry indeed. Contamination meant the sample could not be used in court and Frank had no evidence at all against Gleeson.

'He's going to get away with it, Matron. He's killed Elaine Mackay, left two young boys motherless, ruined who knows how many lives ... I can't believe it's happened!'

'I'm sorry, Sergeant, I really am.'

'*How* did it happen? That's what I need to know.'

'I'm really not sure.'

'Well how do they know it's contaminated at all?'

'For some reason they did two estimations. A dehydrogenous and a gas-chromatography. They're substantially different and the pathologist feels it's the gas-chromatography estimation that's wrong.'

'Meaning?'

'He's blaming the hospital. Which may or may not be right.'

'What else could it be?'

Frank was getting a little aggressive – understandably enough – and Terence stepped in.

'If the sample wasn't kept cool enough, that could have done it. It went by taxi, didn't it, Marta? If Wally Pope was delayed, say …'

'I'll check out that end, then. And I expect you to do the same here.'

Marta flared at that. 'Well of course we will, Sergeant! Do you think I'm happy about this?'

'No. No, of course not. It's the thought of that little … the thought that he could get off scot free … it doesn't bear thinking about.'

Frank left to go and see Wally Pope. Marta sighed. 'If I recall it was Ruth Hammond who took the sample.'

'I'll leave you to it,' Terence said. 'I can't put Ian Sutton off any longer.' They went their separate ways. It was not a good morning for either.

Terence went into Ian's room feigning a cheerfulness he did not feel, asking after his well-being while he checked the traction on his leg. Ian said he'd managed to get some sleep.

'You don't remember having a visitor then?'

'Visitor? No. But then the nurse gave me some pethidine, that stuff knocks me right out.'

'It was long after visiting hours. Andy Mackay came to see you. He was pretty distraught.'

'Yes, well … I didn't know.'

Terence pulled the visitor's chair close to the bed and sat down. 'Ian. Can you imagine what they're saying out there?'

'Oh yes, doctor. Only too well. It's a small country

town full of petty-minded people. That's why we were leaving.'

'Not everyone would agree.'

Ian didn't respond to that. Terence said, 'I understand your loss. The pain you must be feeling. Please don't think I'm trying to make light of your grief. But you can still leave if you want to. You don't have two young boys. And quite obviously your whole life isn't centred on this town.'

'What do you want me to do? Tell Andy it isn't the way they all think? Make up some cock and bull story?'

'I'm asking you to give him back his life, Ian. Let him believe that he still had a wife, that his boys had a mother who loved them.'

'Of course she loved her boys. But Andy? Good old hard-working, solid, down-to-earth Andy? The truth is, he lost her years ago. She loved me. You have no idea how much we loved each other.'

'And you can hold that love close forever, no one can take it away from you.'

'You want me to lie about it.'

'I'm asking you to do a great kindness, do you think that could possibly hurt Elaine? One of the kindest women any of us ever knew? Do you think she wouldn't understand?'

Ian shook his head. 'It's too much.'

'She's dead, Ian. But Andy has to find a way to go on living.'

Terence left, feeling that perhaps he'd been too hard on Ian, that it was all just a ghastly mess, that no one could help whom they fell in love with. And hoping that Frank could still find a way to charge Peter Gleeson.

It was not to be. Marta had talked to Ruth Hammond who had never, as it turned out, taken such a blood sample before. Ruth had described exactly what she had done: she had dutifully swabbed Peter Gleeson's arm with alcohol, drawn up the sample – Marta stopped her there.

'Do you see anything wrong with your actions so far, Ruth?'

Ruth thought about it and suddenly the light dawned. 'Oh my God! I shouldn't have swabbed it! Or I should have made sure it was completely dry ... oh, Matron! I'm so terribly sorry.'

'It's a bit late for that,' Marta said tartly and then, seeing that Ruth was nearly in tears, regretted her tone almost immediately.

'If you want my resignation ...'

Marta sighed. 'There's no need for that. It's my fault too, I should have made sure you understood the procedure. We were rushed and we made mistakes and we're going to pay for them dearly.'

That was certainly true. Not that Frank Gilroy did more than express his displeasure. He knew better than most that honest mistakes got made; one had to accept that and deal with the consequences. So once he knew the blood sample was unusable, he drove straight out to the Gleeson place, a dump on the edge of town with a couple of old car bodies up on blocks in the shed that Peter was supposedly working on. If Peter knew how to work. There was also a number of bee hives in a small orchard, which Arnie Gleeson, Peter's dad and a Vietnam vet, somehow managed to tend.

Peter was talking to a mate on a motor-bike outside the shed when Frank pulled up in the police car and got out. The mate, Jimmy Hall, took one look at Frank and hastily concluded his business. He nodded at Frank.

'Sarge.' The bike, a Yamaha, roared into life and was gone.

'Morning, Gleeson. Where's your dad?'

'Still in bed. Had a bad night.'

Frank looked after the vanishing bike. 'Worrying about the company you keep.'

Peter didn't like the sergeant's tone. Not what you'd call friendly.

'You want something, Sarge?'

Frank sighed as though he bore the weight of the world's sins on his shoulders. Or at least those of Wandin Valley. 'Where shall I begin? But first the good news, Gleeson. You're not going to be charged over the death of Mrs. Mackay.'

Peter couldn't believe it. And made the mistake of getting cocky. 'Told you I hadn't been drinking. Didn't I tell you?'

Frank thought if he decked the little bastard no one would see it. His father in any case would probably approve. But he was too tired and too sick at heart to bother.

'The sample was contaminated, son. The whole town knows you'd been drinking. It doesn't matter what you say, it doesn't matter how much you kid yourself – no one's going to believe you.'

'You reckon that's fair?'

'Oh yes. Absolutely I do.' Frank let it sink in for a minute. 'You know the last time we talked, I thought it might have sunk in a bit. I thought one day you might accept some responsibility for what you've done. But you still seem to think you're getting away with it. But you're not, Peter. Every day, for the rest of your life, you're going to wake up knowing you killed a woman who did nothing but good for this town. Every time you see Chris or Joel Mackay in the street, you'll know they don't have a mother because of you. Heavens, mate, every time you want a meat pie, you'll have to drive to Burrigan!'

He looked towards the house and saw Arnie Gleeson standing in the doorway, leaning on his crutch, an old man in his early forties.

'And your dad'll have to live with it too, Peter, because these things rub off. Like he doesn't have enough to make his life miserable. At least think about it? And think about staying away from Jimmy Hall while you're at it.'

Frank waved to Arnie and drove away with the unshakeable feeling that his words had fallen on the stoniest of ground and nothing would change. He may have felt a little better if he had seen Peter Gleeson some time later sobbing in his father's arms. But whether the repentance which washed over Peter that morning would last, whether he was strong enough to turn his life around – well, it was far too soon to tell.

CHAPTER TWENTY-THREE

Andy MacKay arrived at the hospital and ran into Judy Loveday. 'Can I help you, Mr Mackay?'

'I need to see Ian Sutton. I was told he'd be well enough today.'

'Well yes, but it's not visiting hours yet.'

Marta came out of her office. 'That's alright, sister, I think we can make an exception. I'll take Mr. Mackay around. Oh – there's Mr White ringing – would you?'

'Sure.' Judy went off, not surprised that rules were being broken, under the circumstances.

'I'd like to see him alone,' Andy said.

'Of course. But he was badly injured, I can't allow you to stay too long.'

'I understand. I know where his room is.'

'Yes. I believe you do.'

'I apologise for last night. I was out of my mind.'

'That's alright. Go then. Ten minutes.' Andy thanked her and went to Ian's room. Marta watched him walk off down the corridor and said a little prayer.

Ever since Terence had left him, Ian had tried to work

out what he was going to say. To lie felt like a complete betrayal of all that he and Elaine had meant to each other; a total negation of their love. If he went down that path, he would have to spin a web of falsehoods about a friendship that had been left behind three years ago. He would have to hide his own grief and instead give support and comfort to others. He felt it was more than he could endure. But deep inside, he knew that what Terence Elliott had said was true; after a decent, even a quite short interval, he had the option of going away. He could do that and leave Andy with his life and his pride intact.

Ian looked up and saw his friend standing in the doorway. That is, he saw a shadow of Andy Mackay, grey and drawn and anxious, a drowning man looking for a lifebuoy. Ian made himself smile.

'Andy. This is nice. Come in.'

Andy went in and sat in the visitor's chair. 'How are you going?'

'Getting there. I'll be right. Andy … I didn't know about Elaine until yesterday … I don't know what to say. How are you coping?'

'I'm not, that's the truth of it. They tell me she didn't suffer, I guess that helps a little.' He paused. 'Ian, I know it wasn't your fault. But the stories going round town – the stuff people are saying …'

Ian sighed. 'Yes. I can imagine.'

Andy was finding this impossible. 'The thing is, I need to know the truth. I have to tell my boys the truth. Don't I?'

And that's when Ian accepted that the last thing Andy needed was the truth, he just needed *a* truth, and any one would do. He, Ian, would lie to give it to him.

'They all want to know what Elaine was doing in my car, right?'

'Yes.'

It came to Ian in a flash from some guardian angel. 'Andy, it's your birthday in a couple of weeks. Elaine wanted to organise a lunch for you. And when I said I had to go out to Hicklewhite's Winery, she thought she'd come and we'd check out the restaurant – they did it up recently – and see if it might be nice. It was all going to be a big surprise. Oh, Andy ... I'm so sorry.'

Andy was suddenly the one comforting Ian.

'Not your fault, mate. Not your fault.'

'She was so excited about it ... whatever people are saying, Andy – that's what happened. For God's sake, we've all been friends for so long, how could they think ...?'

'I know, mate. I know. But they do. They'll get over it when they know the truth. Thank God I've still got friends like you.'

Andy stopped for a word with Marta on his way out, to thank her for letting him visit out of hours.

'Ian cleared up a few things,' he said.

'I'm glad. It usually helps.'

'They were going to check out one of the wineries. Elaine was planning a lunch for my birthday. At least I can tell the boys.'

Marta made it her business to give that piece of news to both Shirley and Terence and since they were regarded as impeccable sources, it was gospel by evening. Any suggestion of Ian Sutton and Elaine Mackay running off anywhere was regarded as both tasteless and absurd.

Jenny Secombe heard the revised version of events at the milkbar and was pleased; she'd always liked the Mackays and had had her doubts about the rumours anyway. She just wished her dad had the money to send her away to boarding school like the Mackay boys so she didn't have to put up with morons like Tony Pieri and his mates who were now giving her hell. But she guessed there were morons at every school. It was still stinking hot and she rode home past the waterhole, thinking she might have a swim but Tony was there. He hadn't wasted time in getting a new girlfriend, she noticed. It was Avril Moore, a skinny blonde from Jenny's year. Avril wasn't a bad kid and Jenny thought she deserved a whole lot better than Tony. She watched while Tony chased her to his panel van. She was giggling and screaming. She leapt into the back of the van and Tony leapt after her and pulled the curtain across. Jenny couldn't resist. She rode up to the van and banged on the window.

'Hey, Avril!'

An angry Tony opened it.

'What the hell?'

'Just wondering if Avril's on the pill? Because she's younger than me, you see? And her parents are Catholic like yours, Tony, aren't they? Has he asked you yet, Avril? 'Cause he will, you can bet on it! Nothing matters but that little thing between his legs! Just a friendly warning!'

And she rode off laughing, feeling quite empowered and at peace with the world and thinking she must call and say a big thank you to Vicky Dean.

Frank Gilroy called in at the Dean house that evening. Shirley hadn't been home from work for long and offered him tea, since she was making one.

'I usually begin with tea, it delays the start of drinking a bit.'

'Why, have you got a problem with it?'

'With alcohol? Good heavens no, Frank, I was joking. Though mind you there are times – like the last few days – when I could easily develop one.'

'It's been tough all round. Though I reckon the worst

might be over.'

'We've still got a funeral to get through.'

'Sometimes that can be quite a relief.'

'True.'

They nattered until Shirley brought the tea to the table.

'Thanks,' Frank said, and then: 'Ian Sutton's a good bloke.'

'Yes.'

'Did you give the bag to Andy?'

'Yes. He wanted me to have it but I said it was much too soon to start giving things away.'

'Very wise.'

'Frank … no, just a minute.' She got up and went to her own handbag and retrieved an envelope from it and went and sat back down again.

'I hope you're not going to be very cross.'

'Why would I be cross, Shirl?'

'I – intercepted a letter. This letter.'

'Oh yes.'

'Which I found in Elaine's handbag. It's addressed to Andy but she never got a chance to post it.'

Frank took the letter and examined it and handed it back. 'It hasn't been franked. It's not Her Majesty's Mail until it's franked. At least I don't think it is, I'd have to check.'

'So it wouldn't be a crime to destroy it.'

'More of a crime, I think, to ruin the good work that's been done today.'

'It's such a relief that you feel that way, Frank.' She ripped the letter across several times and put it in the bin. Frank appeared not to notice.

'Good cuppa, Shirl.'

The rain came the day they buried Elaine. A front had been building all week, moving slowly across the state until it finally reached the north-east on Thursday morning. The town was full. Elaine was well-known and well-loved and highly respected, and friends came from hundreds of kilometres away, even from Sydney and Melbourne. As Bob Hatfield said to Vernon Locke, as they strove to get the club ready for the luncheon after the service, it was bigger than *Ben Hur*. At least by Wandin Valley standards. Big maybe but sad as such an occasion always is, when someone is taken before their time, leaving young children to grieve for them.

The town closed for the morning but hospitals can't close. Brendan had offered to work so Marta could attend the service and Molly came in to help in the kitchen. They watched the long funeral procession pass in pouring rain from the hospital verandah. Others watched through their windows: Sandra Myers, with her husband and baby daughter; Norah Bird, thinking it could be her time soon, though surely God knew Bruce couldn't manage without her. Ian Sutton, who was still in traction, couldn't even get to the window but lay alone and wept for his lost love.

When it was all over, Andy Mackay took his boys home and his family and a few close friends, Shirley Dean among them, talked of Elaine through the day and into the night and began the long process of learning to live without her.

The next day, all over the valley, life began to return to normal as it must. Over breakfast, Molly tackled Brendan about the rats.

'We have to do something.'

'Can't we just cohabit?'

'With *rats*?'

'They might be some sort of little native rat.'

'Nah. I checked with Vicky. Possibly Norwegian rats.'

'Poor little things. So far from home.'

'They've got nothing to do with Norway. It's just a name.'

'Okay, look, my first day off – which was yesterday – I'll put some poison up there.'

'Thanks, darling.' Molly munched on some toast. 'Wasn't it nice, yesterday. The way the whole town closed.'

'I asked the matron about that. It's a country thing, it always happens.'

'You wouldn't see it in the city. Too worried about losing a dollar.'

'True.'

'Rats or no rats – I like it here.'

'Yeah. Me too.'

While Molly and Brendan were beginning to some small degree to settle into the rhythms of their new life, Simon Bowen was becoming increasingly discontented with his. He could not put his finger on the cause; well not entirely. He was honest enough to admit that it had quite a lot to do with some news he'd received from his mother. He also felt it was somehow tied up with the pace of rural life, some days the slowness and sameness of it just got to him. And then there was Vicky Dean, she got to him too. Well he'd just have to make an effort to change things. Starting with his wretched accommodation. He made a note to phone the agent about the house in Bligh Street.

But by Friday things were no better. The house in Bligh Street had gone and Vicky had knocked him back once again.

'Just a meal, Vicky. Pleasant conversation. Your choice of subject. I'm lonely, goddamn it.'

'Sorry. I really can't go anywhere. There's this horse, belongs to the Thompsons – I don't know what's wrong with it, I'm bound to get called out.' Simon didn't push it. If he was hurt, he wasn't going to show it. After he'd gone, Vicky did wonder why she always said no.

That had been at lunchtime. Late in the day, Simon had seen his last patient – he was getting just a few now – and was sitting in his surgery wondering what to do for the evening when Terence popped his head in.

'Sorry I can't have a drink tonight, I'm off to Melbourne.'

'No worries.'

'Got any plans for the weekend?'

'Not really.'

'Is something wrong, Simon? Shirley's worried about you.'

'I'm fine. Consumed with professional jealousy, that all.'

'Oh?'

'Just heard that a mate has scored a job as a registrar at RPA.'

'What speciality?'

'Dermatology.'

'You want to be a dermatologist?'

'No. But compared to what I'm doing …'

'I don't believe I'm hearing this. After the week you've had. Your friend's involved in major surgery, is he?'

'I guess not.'

Terence felt for Simon; he understood the pressure Simon had been under all through medical school, to do as well as the rest of his family, and how bitter it must have felt when he had not quite succeeded.

'Simon, you're clever, you care, you'll be a great GP. And you'll save just as many lives as your mate. Or the rest of your brilliant family. Just remember that. I've got to go. Get some rest, the fruit pickers start arriving next week, we'll have our work cut out then.'

Simon, feeling a fraction better, followed him out. 'Why?'

'They're itinerants, most of them. No regular health care. Rotten life.'

'No romance in the open road then?'

'Not on those wages.'

'Right. Well enjoy the big smoke.'

Terence left, carrying Elaine Mackay's suitcase. Simon waited till he'd gone then looked at Shirley.

'A lady's suitcase?'

'Just some stuff for St Vinnie's, Simon. Don't ask.'

Simon put two and two together quickly enough and nodded.

'There was a call for you,' Shirley said. 'The estate agent. The house in Bligh Street's still available after all. He said they're open till six.'

That, at least, was good news. 'I might go round there now, then. Of course it's probably a dump.'

'I know that house. It's rather nice, I think you'd like it.'

'Alright, I will go.'

'And the rest of the weekend?'

Simon suddenly decided if Vicky preferred the company of horses he may as well try it too. 'I'm going to ring my cousins.'

'Cousins?'

'The polo-playing Smythe-Kings. Got that huge place out past Magnolia Vale, my mother's been at me to get in touch. I haven't seen them in years but I'm sure we'll get on just fine, Vicky can't stand them. 'Night, Shirl.' He gave her a wave and was gone.

Oh, dear, Shirley thought. So it's still Vicky. She hadn't realised his feelings were that strong, she'd thought it was all just a bit of fun. Simon Bowen and Vicky Dean? She didn't have to consult the tea leaves to see trouble ahead.

EPILOGUE

It was a calm, still evening as Terence drove out of town. Already there was a faint tinge of green beside the road and the coolness in the air spoke of autumn days ahead. Proper autumn, Terence thought, not late, baking summer.

He thought back over the past week, the safe arrival of Sandra Myers' baby daughter, so quickly followed by Elaine's tragic death. Talk about life's rich tapestry. He'd taken some small steps to recovery himself but there was, he knew, still a long way to go.

He stopped the car at the Eldershaw vineyard. Not a lot of grapes, no, but those that were there looked alright. Big, fat bunches, quality rather than quantity. What a loving owner could do with that place. He had a meeting with his solicitor tomorrow morning. But first there was tonight to think about. He'd promised to be in St Kilda in time for a late dinner, he'd better get going. He put the Nissan Patrol into gear and headed south.

A COUNTRY PRACTICE BOOK 2

Continuing the story of the country folk of Wandin Valley … Enjoy a preview of the first chapter of the next book in the *A Country Practice* series of novels.

The long, hot summer was over and autumn had come at last to Wandin Valley. Golden willows lined the creeks; in the paddocks, dotted amongst the ubiquitous gums, the reds and yellows of oak and elm and chestnut glowed brightly, while all along Mrs Harriet Eldershaw's drive, her beeches blazed like a bushfire. You had to give it to the early settlers, their nostalgia for distant climes had improved the landscape considerably – that is, if one overlooked the undergrowth, choked as it so often was with hawthorn and blackberries and Paterson's Curse.

Terence Elliot was admiring the beeches now from Harriet's shaded verandah where the two of them were having afternoon tea. The pot was silver, the scones were delicious, the sponge cake perfection. Were it not for the aforementioned gumtrees, and the rows of grapevines marching away in ordered rows before him,

Terence felt he could have been at some English country house, albeit one in need of some repair. The effect was heightened every time Harriet spoke, for although she'd been in Victoria for nearly half a century, she had never quite lost those Home County vowels. Terence had known her for some time, though they weren't close – she was far too healthy to often require the services of a doctor. He wished he'd had the chance to gain her friendship.

'I'm glad autumn's come at last,' Harriet said. 'I wanted to see my beech trees in all their glory one last time.' She smiled. 'Your beech trees now.'

'Let's share them, shall we?' said Terence. 'You know you'll be welcome to visit any time. And they're not really mine for another month.'

'That's what I wanted to talk to you about, Terence. The packers are coming in two days, I'm putting everything into storage and I'm taking off. I've booked a flight to England and I don't know when I'll be back.'

'You've still got family there?'

'A sister and several cousins. I haven't seen them for ten years.'

'Then it's time you went.'

'The thing is, the grapes are the best they've been for years – someone should keep an eye on them until vintage. Someone besides the silvereyes, that is, the wretched creatures have already had more than their fair share.'

'Those beautiful fake owls you've got don't work then?'

'A minor deterrent only. You should think about netting next year, it's really the only solution but it is hard work. Anyway, I thought perhaps we could come to some arrangement ... you pay a peppercorn rent until settlement and take over straightaway. What do you think?'

'That you're a far-sighted and generous woman, Harriet.'

'I can't abide waste. You agree then?'

'I do. Though I can't guarantee I'll be able to make wine this year. I've got a lot to learn.'

'Sell the grapes to Ian Jamieson, he makes a decent cabernet. And he'll pay you in kind if you like.'

'Sounds like a win-win.'

'For all of us. I'm so glad you bought this place. I know it needs a lot of work and people will no doubt tell you you're quite mad to take it on but I'm sure that in time you'll bring it back to its former glory.'

'I'll certainly do my best, Harriet.'

'And you'll succeed. You'll fall in love with the place, as I did all those years ago. A moment.' She disappeared through the French doors and returned with a small tray holding an old bottle and two small crystal glasses. She uncorked the bottle and poured the amber liquid.

'Lester's last tokay.' She passed one to Terence. 'Shall we drink a toast, then? New beginnings for both of us.'

'To new beginnings.'

The tokay was delicious, smooth and mellow. Terence hoped it was a harbinger of things to come. He hoped that Harriet's trip back to the land of her birth would bring her much pleasure. And he hoped that he himself was not indeed quite mad in taking on this lovely but very run-down old vineyard.

While the grapes were not yet ready to be picked, Wandin Valley was gearing itself up for the apple harvest. This annual event divided the town into two camps. There were those who regarded it as a blessing – mainly, it must be said, on economic grounds. On the other side were those who – lacking a certain tolerance –

would have all the pickers arrested on sight. Even while Terence Elliot was enjoying his tea with Harriet Eldershaw, the matter was being rehashed in the local post office. Esme Watson had the floor. Esme, it transpired, had passed a broken-down car on her way back from Burrigan and had failed to stop and render assistance.

'I'm sure I know my Christian duty,' she said, 'but really, I was just too frightened to stop. If I'd had someone with me, then maybe – but I was all alone. A single woman. What if they'd attacked me?'

'*Attacked* you, Miss Watson?' Molly Jones sounded as though she could hardly imagine anything less probable.

'There were three of them, Molly. Three pickers. Well, two I suppose. One was a child.'

'And this child was going to attack you if you stopped to offer help?'

'They looked like gypsies. They can't be trusted. That's all I'm saying.'

Molly rolled her eyes and paid for her stamps. 'I'm sure the pickers bring quite a bit of money to the town, don't they?' she asked innocently.

'They do indeed,' said Ida Dugdale, the postmistress, who was very much in favour of the itinerants. 'Don't do you any harm either, do they, Andy?' Andy Mackay owned the local bakery. His pies were legendary. He smiled agreement.

'My profits go up by fifteen percent.'

'There are more important things than money!' snapped Esme. 'You ask Sergeant Gilroy how he feels about this – this invasion. About the increase in crime! You just wait until some defenceless woman is violated in her bed!' And much put out, Miss Watson left.

'Poor love,' Molly said, not entirely without sympathy. 'She seems to have an absolute thing about the pickers, doesn't she? I wonder why?'

Liz Anderson, the principal of the local primary school, decided it was time to have her say. 'Well it's not their fault, but they do cause a huge problem for the school.'

'How, Liz? What do they do?' Andy asked.

Liz laughed. 'They turn up! Or the kids do. Andy said his profits go up by fifteen percent – well so do my class sizes. Trouble is, we don't get any extra funding so I can't employ another teacher. As well as that, the kids are from all over, from interstate, they're all at different levels – it's challenging, to say the least. But we've just got to make the best of it – the fruit has to be picked.'

'Either that or we leave it to the cockatoos,' said Andy. 'I swear I've never seen such big flocks of them. Biding their time, just waiting to swoop.'

'Tell me about it,' Molly sighed. 'They got all our plums, left me just enough for two tiny jars of jam. I'm for the pickers, they can be my avenging angels.'

A huge flock of those very cockatoos rose screeching from the nearby paddock as Bill Ferguson pulled his ute off the road. A battered old station-wagon had broken down; an elderly man, a young woman and a small boy stood beside it. They did not look like avenging angels. Poor sods, thought Bill and went to see if he could lend a hand. Unlike Esme Watson, Bill did not see every fruit-picker as a potential serial killer.

'G'day,' he said. 'What seems to be the trouble?'

The man came forward to meet him. 'Thank you so much for stopping. It is, I think, old age. Mine, that is. We have a flat tyre but I cannot get the nuts off to remove it.'

Bill sensed the old man's discomfort in asking for help, or appearing vulnerable. He had quite a strong accent, middle European maybe, but his English was good, his manner self-deprecating. The woman seemed wary, she kept an arm around the child and watched intently. Bill smiled in sympathy, trying to put them all at ease.

'Like me to have a go?' he said. 'They can be a bugger sometimes. Oh, I'm Bill, by the way. Bill Ferguson. Got a farm up the road a bit.'

'Alex Popovich,' the old man said. 'This is my daughter-in-law … my grandson.' But he did not give their names. He handed Bill the shifter and took him round to the passenger side. It was the rear wheel. The jack looked even older than the car and not fit to bear its weight. Bill was glad that he did not need to get underneath. The nuts were indeed tight and it took all his strength to get them off but eventually the job was done and the tyre, which was badly damaged, came off. Alex Popovich had the spare out, waiting. It was not, Bill noticed, in very good shape.

'Where are you going to be picking?' he asked as he got it into position.

'Cameron's,' said Popovich.

'Oh yeah,' said Bill, non-committal but thinking, God help them. 'Been there before?' Popovich just nodded.

'I guess you don't get much say,' Bill said.

'You do not. But the boss – I mean the gang boss – he is a good man.'

'Well I suppose that counts for a lot. There you go, then.' He was about to leave it at that, he'd done his good deed, he thought he should probably go and let these people get on with their lives. But he could feel the little boy staring at him, he knew the child had watched his every move. He sensed too that this little family had known better times, they had not always had to drive a beaten-up Holden from job to job.

'Tell you what,' Bill said. 'I used to have a wagon like this. Sold her a while back. But I reckon I've still got a couple of decent tyres. And you're going to need a new spare. I'll hunt them out, bring one out to you.'

Finally the young woman spoke up. 'We couldn't let you do that. Could we, Dad?'

But Alex didn't get a chance to speak. 'Just cluttering the place up,' Bill said. He smiled again, a slow, conspiratorial smile. 'Hey, I reckon anyone brave enough to work for Bruce Cameron deserves a break. See you in a day or two.' He ambled back to his ute, gave them a wave and drove off. The little boy looked after him, awestruck, waving back till he was out of sight.

'Do you reckon he meant it?' the woman, Silvia, said.

Alex just shrugged. A long hard life had taught him not to count on anything. 'We'd better get going, we don't want Robbo to think we are not coming.'

They arrived at Bruce Cameron's orchard half an hour later. Cameron was talking to Robbo, who had hired the gang of pickers as he did every year. Alex got out of the car to report their arrival. Robbo greeted him warmly; not so Bruce Cameron.

'Not you again,' was what he said. He turned to Robbo. 'You never mentioned the Popoviches.'

'On the list, Bruce. Good workers, too.'

'You reckon?'

Robbo gave him a long look, daring him to make an issue of it. 'Can we just see how it goes?'

'Got to fill their quota like everyone else,' Cameron said and he walked off.

'We won't let you down, Robbo.'

'I know, mate. Staying at the camp park?' Alex nodded. Robbo went with him back to the wagon and stuck his head in the window to speak to Silvia. 'Silvia.'

'Hello, Robbo.'

'Hey, Lexy. Going to school this year?' Lexy shook his head.' Robbo glanced at Silvia, surprised.

'He's not been well. I might let him wait till next year.'

'Won't do any harm. See you tomorrow, then.' He gave the little boy a Mintie he pulled from his pocket and went to meet some more arrivals.

Silvia let out a long breath. 'Here we go again, Dad. One more apple harvest.'

But for Silvia, this would be a harvest like no other and several lives, her own included, would be changed forever before it ended.

A Country Practice Book 2 is published in paperback and as an ebook from Amazon in September 2015.

Read more about the series at
www.acountrypractice.info

ABOUT THE AUTHOR

Judith Colquhoun was born in Queensland and grew up in Sydney. She studied production at the National Institute of Dramatic Art and soon after graduating, love and a job at the ABC took her to Melbourne. There she learnt to drink coffee, wear black and follow St Kilda in the AFL. Later, she lived in London for a time, spent many years in country Victoria and long enough in Italy to fall in love with the Mezzogiorno. She is now back in Melbourne and may even stay there.

She started writing when she was six and from the age of twenty-three has always earned her living from it in one way or another. She was a scriptwriter for far too long, writing countless hours of television for many of Australia's most popular shows. Her output included one hundred episodes of *A Country Practice*.

Judith has worked as an editor and script producer and in Italy was a script consultant on the serial *Un Posto Al Sole*. She has won five Awgie Awards and in 2007 was made a Life Member of the Australian Writers' Guild.

In 2009 she finally gave up scriptwriting to attempt a novel. *Thicker Than Water*, which is largely set in southern Italy, was published in 2014. It was Highly Commended in the Fellowship of Australian Writers 2014 National Literary Awards.

Judith is married with two children and three grandchildren.

20236839R00129

Printed in Great Britain
by Amazon